MICHELLE VERNAL LIVES in Christchurch, New Zealand with her husband, two teenage sons and attention seeking tabby cats, Humphrey and Savannah. Before she started writing novels, she had a variety of jobs:

Pharmacy shop assistant, girl who sold dried up chips and sausages at a hot food stand in a British pub, girl who sold nuts (for 2 hours) on a British market stall, receptionist, P.A...Her favourite job though is the one she has now – writing stories she hopes leave her readers with a satisfied smile on their face.

If you'd like to know when Michelle's next book is coming out you can visit her website at: www.michellevernalbooks.com

Also by Michelle Vernal

The Cooking School on the Bay

Second-hand Jane

Staying at Eleni's

The Traveller's Daughter

Sweet Home Summer

When We Say Goodbye

And...

The Guesthouse on the Green Series

Book 1 - O'Mara's

Book 2 – Moira-Lisa Smile

Book 3 –What goes on Tour

Book 4 – Rosi's Regrets

Book 5 – Christmas at O'Mara's

Book 6 – A Wedding at O'Mara's

Book 7 – Maureen's Song

Book 8 – The O'Maras in LaLa Land

Book 9 – Due in March

Book 10 – A Baby at O'Mara's – out May 2021

Isabel's Story two book series

The Promise

The Letter

The Bestselling Liverpool Brides Series

The Autumn Posy

The Winter Posy

The Spring Posy – out August 2021

What Goes on Tour

By Michelle Vernal

Chapter 1

Dublin Airport was a hive of activity, full of people with places to go and people to see. A sea of bobbing heads striding around importantly, hefting bags about, wheeling cases behind them or pushing luggage-laden trolleys. There was a buzz in the air and it was infectious making Moira feel important as she strode toward the check in desk or rather shuffled toward it. She was bent double by her backpack, a turtle with its house on its back. How those poor creatures carted that weight around day in day out was beyond her and she was beginning to wonder if she'd overdone it on the packing.

Moira had packed for every possible climatic event. The guide book Mammy had bought and given her to read said it was cooler in the north of Vietnam than the south. She hadn't wanted to take any chances with the retail outlets on offer once on foreign soil. She didn't know much about the shopping situation in Vietnam but she was fairly certain there'd be no Marks and Spencer or Penneys finest where she was going. Hence, she'd opted to stuff her pack with everything from bikinis and flip-flops through to thermals and hiking boots. The hardest decision had been not packing one single pair of heels, not even her casually, dressy ones. She didn't think she'd gone a whole day in flats since she was at school but this definitely wasn't going to be a high-heeled sort of a holiday.

The backpack wasn't hers either. This encumbrance weighing her down belonged to Lisa the no-frills Australian legal secretarial temp at Mason Price where Moira was employed as a receptionist. She'd offered her the loan of it when she'd gotten wind of Moira's upcoming trip assuring her she'd find it much easier to manage getting on and off buses than lugging a suitcase about. It had been very generous of her and Moira had felt quite intrepid laying it open on her bed deciding where to put what in its many compartments. She'd left her packing to the last minute as per usual.

Now, feeling the straps pinch her shoulders she'd put money on Lisa not being a subscriber to the O'Mara family travel policy. Mammy was a firm believer in not being caught short. She'd drummed it into her four children to always take two pairs of smalls for every single day they were away and then a few extra sets just in case. Lisa, Moira had decided, was likely to be one of those practical types who'd wash her knickers out at the end of the day, leaving them to dry overnight.

The art of travelling lightly was not something any of the O'Mara's had mastered, not even Patrick. Mind, he had a suit collection that put Aisling's designer shoes to shame and more in the way of hair products and skin potions than any of his sisters. Having said that Moira *had* packed a giant bottle of Evian mineral water spray in her carry-on; her friend Tessa had recommended it to stop her skin drying out. It wasn't that she was vain, it was just she couldn't be doing with flaky skin. Patrick was a vain man. Not a ray of sunshine was allowed to caress his handsome features unless he'd slathered on his SPF 30.

It rankled that Pat hadn't been in touch to wish her and Mammy a good trip. For Mammy's sake as much as hers. He was her golden boy, after all. Her only boy come to that. Fair enough he was in LA but a phone call wasn't too much to ask—five minutes of his precious time. She'd taken off the rose-tinted glasses she'd always worn where her elder brother was concerned these last few months. She'd not liked the way he'd behaved when Aisling had told Mammy she'd take over the running of O'Mara's. It had been obvious he wanted the family guesthouse sold; the proceeds divvied between them so he could focus on whatever it was he was actually doing over there in the city of Angels. Most of all though his lack of contact at a time when she'd needed him most had hurt.

Vain git. She gave him and his obsessive SPF habit a metaphorical flick as she heard Mammy's strident cry behind her. 'Aisling, Moira! I'm after forgetting my passport.'

Christ on a bike, the holiday was off to a grand start.

Chapter 2

M oira swore softly under her breath and came to a halt. She teetered forward as she swung around, narrowly avoiding taking Aisling out in the process.

'You're a menace, with that thing so you are,' Aisling muttered, putting out a steadying hand as she glared at her sister before turning her attention to Mammy.

Maureen O'Mara was patting down the pockets, of which there were many, in her new travel pants. She too had a pack strapped to her back, only hers was brand new and a more compact design than Moira's; it also had a lot of compartments. Plenty in which to lose a passport. Unlike, Moira's pack though, her mammy's wasn't bulging at the seams. Watching her now, Moira couldn't stop thinking of the musical Joseph and the Amazing Technicolour Dream Coat, only it had morphed into Mammy and her Pants of Many Pockets.

'Breathe, Mammy, breathe,' Aisling soothed. 'C'mon now it'll be somewhere on your person. You checked it off your list before we left, remember?' The checklist had been gone through twice to avoid dramas precisely like this one.

'So I did.' Maureen O'Mara took big gulping, calming breaths like Roisin had shown her on her last trip home. *Like you're eating the air, Mammy*. She'd needed to attempt this particular breathing exercise after she'd gotten the bill for the lunch she'd treated her eldest daughter to. She had expensive tastes did Roisin. It came from living in London—the big smoke.

'Mammy have you checked your bum bag?' Moira was impatient, keen to join the line. The sooner they checked in the sooner she could get this pack off her back.

'Moira, I wish you wouldn't call it that, it sounds so undignified.' Nevertheless Maureen lifted her new quick-dry top to reveal the black bag strapped around her waist, unzipping and thrusting her hand inside it to triumphantly hold the little book aloft a beat later.

Moira cut her off before she could launch into the Thanksgiving prayer and they were mistaken for travelling evangelists. 'Jaysus, Mammy, would you cover yourself! I can see your tummy and that's undignified, so it is,' she hissed before carefully turning to make her way over to the ever-growing British Airways queue.

They were flying with the airline to Heathrow where they had to pick up their bags and check in with Thai International for the long haul through to Ho Chi Minh. It meant hanging around Heathrow for a few hours but it had been their cheapest option. By the time they reached the smiley check-in woman with her pillbox hat tilted just so, Maureen O'Mara had told twenty-five strangers she was after having a Mammy and daughter adventure in Vietnam. She'd also informed them that she had six pockets in her travel pants—*six pockets, sure wasn't that a marvellous thing?* Moira knew it was twenty-five people because she'd counted.

Now, she began going through the motions of checking in, cringing at the sight of her passport photo. It was a mug shot, not a photograph. She couldn't blame the smiley woman with a name badge that said she was called Ciara for narrowing her heavily made-up eyes as she glanced down at the photo and then back up at Moira. She did look guilty in it. Whatever her thoughts though, she let it go and passed the little book back to her.

'You look very smart in your uniform,' Maureen beamed pushing past her daughter to take her place at the counter. Moira moved aside watching as her pack was swallowed up by the rubber flaps, satisfied it was on its way to being loaded aboard the plane. Aisling helped her mammy off with her pack and put it down on the scales. Ciara beamed back at Mammy.

She had lipstick on her teeth Moira noted, ignoring the sharp-eyed glance she got as Mammy compared her youngest child with the glamorous woman busy stamping her boarding pass. Moira had thrown on joggers and a sweat top, going for comfort over fashion for their journey. She might have a reputation as the last of the big spenders in the O'Mara family but even she drew the line at forking out shedloads for travel pants. So what if they could be dried in a couple of minutes? Sure, they were bound to have a laundromat somewhere over there and she'd been adamant she did not need six pockets. Nobody needed six pockets! Mammy begged to differ but more to the point the pants were fugly (fecking ugly) in Moira's humble opinion.

'That's a lovely photo of you,' Ciara said to Maureen before snapping her passport shut and handing it back.

Maureen puffed up peacock-like and looked set to launch into a long and involved story as to how she'd managed to get such a fetching passport photo taken. Moira, however, was having none of it and she linked her arm firmly through her mammy's, smiling her thanks at Ciara as she dragged her away.

'Don't rush me, Moira.'

'There's other people waiting, Mammy. Yer woman doesn't need to hear about how if you hold your chin up just so it makes you look younger in photos or whatever it was you were going to tell her. She's a job to be getting on with. There was a queue a mile long waiting to check in.'

Mammy made a tsking noise. 'Well let them wait, I say. People are in too much of a hurry these days, so they are. The art of polite of conversation is being lost and I for one think it's a crying shame.'

Moira cast an exasperated glance over at Aisling who was smirking. She didn't need to be able to read her sister's mind to know it was at the thought of Moira and Mammy sharing a room for nearly a month. The thought made her shudder! Three and a half weeks alone together and not one drop of alcohol was to pass her lips during that time either! There'd be no fuzzy glow to hide behind because she'd be, had been, stone cold sober since Mammy had more or less ordered her on this trip and put the kibosh on her drinking. It was her penance; not in so many words but Mammy was a woman whose face said it all, for the pickle she'd gotten into with a man she'd no right to be carrying on with.

She felt the familiar pang of loneliness mingled with longing she always felt when she thought of Michael. One thing she'd realised though was Mammy was right in so much that hitting the bottle was not the answer. All the things she didn't want to think about, Michael, Daddy not being here anymore, they didn't magically disappear with each drink, they were still there the morning after. The pounding of her head only serving to make her pain worse.

It had been nice to wake up clear-headed this last while. For the first time in a long while she felt like she had some semblance of control over her life. She'd have to survive this trip with Mammy though because she had her date with Tom to look forward to when she got home. She liked him and wanted to see where that took her. He also got two very big ticks in the potential new boyfriend department. One on account of his outstanding bum and the second because he was a nice guy. He had to be because only a nice guy would bother to ask a girl out who'd led him on only to turn him down because her head was all over the place.

Right now though, a meal with Tom to tell him all about this mental trip she was going on, seemed ever such a long way away. Oh yes, it was going to be a tough test getting through this tour of duty with Mammy. Speaking of whom, she noticed she was delving into one of her pockets. A tick later she produced a crumpled tissue and gave a tell-tale sniff. 'Go now while you can,' Moira mouthed at Aisling. Mammy was not good at goodbyes. They were only going on holiday, not emigrating, but she knew from past experience Maureen O'Mara would look like a panda bear, thanks to the non-waterproof mascara she insisted was the only one that didn't make her eyes itch, by the time she disappeared through those gates.

Aisling should know better too than to wait around, what with the number of goodbyes she'd said over the years. Her job in resort management had taken her all around the world until she'd put her roots back down in Dublin to take over the running of the family guesthouse, O'Mara's. Instead of wishing them a happy holiday and saying a quick goodbye however, she was busy rummaging in her shoulder bag.

'I've something for you,' she said to Moira.

Chapter 3

'Is it drugs?' Moira asked receiving the sharp end of Mammy's elbow. She rubbed at her ribs. 'What was that for? Sure, it was only a joke.'

'It's not funny, Moira. You never know who's listening.'

'It's not drugs, Mammy.' Aisling rolled her eyes before retrieving a scrunched-up bundle of material and thrusting it at her sister.

'Yes, but the walls have ears and we might be targeted by the Custom's man if they hear the 'd' word.' She made the inverted comma sign with her fingers.

'Oh for fecks sake, Ash, you loaned her the film, didn't you? After I said not to.'

'Bangkok Hilton's a great film, so it is.' Aisling was defensive. 'And, neither of you are exactly worldly. I let her watch it for educational purposes. Jaysus, Mammy would be the first to put her hand up if someone asked her to carry their bags or a stuffed toy through customs for them especially if they were nice to her.'

'Oh no, I wouldn't, not after seeing that film. Yer Kidman woman deserved an Oscar so she did.' Maureen piped up momentarily distracted from the tears she was working up to by the turn the conversation had taken.

'See.' Aisling shot her sister an 'I was right' look and then remembering what she held in her hand she jiggled the bundle.

'C'mon take them. Don't leave me standing here waving them at you like an eejit.'

Moira did so shaking the fabric out and holding it up. She stared uncomprehendingly at a pair of baggy elasticized waist and bottomed pants. They had elephants all over them and looked like something a clown might wear. 'What the feck are these?'

'Elephant pants,' Aisling said. She'd debated whether or not to give them to her sister. They were the sort of thing that would look ridiculous if she were to strut down O'Connell Street in them but in the middle of Asia, they'd look right at home. 'I bought them when I was in Thailand. Everyone wears them and they're super light and comfortable.'

'Like my fisherman pants,' Maureen piped up. She'd opted not to wear them on the flight deciding on her six pocket, travel pair instead. It wasn't just because they wouldn't crease but because she didn't fancy her chances of getting the fisherman ones done up in the airplane toilets. It would be too much of a challenge in such close quarters and she'd decided the odds were too high of her smacking her head on the toilet door as she bent down to pull the back bit up through to the front—a complicated business. A concussion was not on the cards for this holiday, thanks very much!

'They have elephants all over them.' Moira screwed her nose up. 'And I'm going to Vietnam not Thailand. They don't have elephants there, do they?' She'd been wary when Mammy had first informed her she was heading to Asia of hippopotamuses. They were, according to the television show she'd seen recently, among the world's most deadly creatures. She now knew there was no chance of bumping into one of them but elephants? Well she wasn't one hundred per cent. She'd have to look it up in the guide book.

'Look, Moira, you won't care whether they're covered in teddy bears once you hit the tropics. Those pants are light enough to wear despite the heat and they'll stop your thighs rubbing together and your legs getting eaten alive.' Aisling was indignant her gift wasn't being well received, although she knew she shouldn't be surprised; graciousness was not one of her sister's stronger personality traits.

'My thighs do not rub together!'

'Believe me, Moira, in that heat your thighs will slap together. Kate Moss's thighs would rub together.'

'Girls, stop bickering. I've brought the Lanacane gel, nobody's thighs will be rubbing or slapping together under my watch.'

Moira shook her head; it was one of those surreal life moments. Here she was in the airport discussing elephant pants and chafing. It was hardly the stuff of Hello Magazine, where the celebs, ie aforementioned Kate Moss, all strode out of Arrivals looking amazing, a pair of big black glasses covering their faces and the kind of tight-fitting jeans sprayed on that Mammy always said would give a girl a nasty bout of thrush, especially if she were to sit in them for thirteen hours straight.

'Take the pants, Moira, and say thank you to your sister. It was very thoughtful of her so it was.'

Moira grudgingly did as she was told even though she knew she wouldn't be seen dead in them. She shoved them inside her carry-on bag while Mammy yanked Aisling toward her quick dry top. She hugged her daughter to her ample bosom and began to sniffle.

'Mammy, stop that.' Aisling's voice was muffled. 'I'll be fine. I've got Quinn to look after me remember?'

'Ah, he's a lovely lad, so he is.' The words and a grand son-in-law he'd make me hung in the air.

'Don't you be moving him in while I'm away,' Moira muttered pulling her sister from her mammy's arms to give her a hug goodbye. 'Because I plan on coming back.'

'I plan on you coming back too.' Aisling squeezed her sister back, although, it would be nice spending each and every night with him for the next month, because moving him in while her sister was away was exactly what she was planning on doing. She knew he was at his mam's this very minute packing his bag. 'Look after each other,' she called as Moira hauled Mammy toward the sliding doors. 'And keep in touch. Promise me you won't be riding on any of those scooters over there, Mammy?'

'I promise. We promise, don't we, Moira?' Maureen paused to call back.

Moira gave her sister the Girl Guide salute. 'I promise to do my very best.'

Aisling didn't grin, another panicked thought had sprung to mind. 'Mammy you remembered to sort your insurance out, didn't you?'

Mammy gave her the thumbs up and a final wave before the doors slid shut behind them.

Aisling stood there for a moment feeling odd. That was it then, they were gone. It had always been her that had done the leaving. This was a first and, sending up a silent prayer that her mam and sister travel safely, she turned and made her way toward the exit. Quinn would be waiting at home for her. The thought warmed her and chased away the feeling of trepidation watching them walk though those doors had left her with. Five minutes later as she eyed the ticket under the windshield wiper, she was too busy cursing the parking warden to worry about Mammy and Moira. There went the new pair of Manolo's she'd had her eye on.

Chapter 4

Mammy dabbed at her eyes with the tissue that looked like it had seen better days as she stood on the other side of passport control. They'd emerged in the glitzy duty free area having passed inspection without incident despite Moira's dodgy picture. Moira suspected this was down to the customs officer man's sixth sense. An ability to size people up must be in their job description because she was sure he'd known were he to give Maureen a conversational opening he'd live to regret it.

As it was Mammy had drawn breath, her chest puffing up magnificently beneath that quick-dry fabric. She was all set to tell him why she was teary over leaving the country even if it was only for a holiday, how it was a mammy's lot in life. He must have guessed too it would be followed swiftly by questioning along the lines of how it was a nice young man like himself, had come to be working on customs and did he catch many drug dealers? Hence, he'd slammed her passport shut, thrust it back at her and waved them both through, Mammy sniffing all the way, partly from indignation and partly because it was just what she did.

Now, Maureen O'Mara's tears miraculously dried as she spied the perfume section. A child in a sweet shop. Mind, thought Moira, a certain serum she'd been unable to justify the price of at Boots might just be affordable tax free. Oh, and there was that bottle of Allure by Chanel she'd been hankering after. She'd had to make do for months with a sneaky spray of

Aisling's Gucci. Personally it wasn't Moira's favourite but needs must. Where was the harm in checking them out? Hadn't her credit card just received its minimum repayment? Sure it was raring to go.

'Ooh, I do like a free squirt so I do, come on, Moira.'

She was like a bee to honey, and Moira followed her as she honed in, her nose twitching as she sought out her go-to fragrance.

'Mammy, why don't you try something new? Live dangerously, come on. Look at them all, there's hundreds to choose from.' To demonstrate her point she picked up the bottle of Jean Paul Gaultier that was closest to hand. Maureen blinked at the womanly shaped bottle with its gold cone bra, corset embellishment.

'I don't think so, Moira. I couldn't be doing with that. I'd think of what's-her-name every time I picked it up.'

'Madonna?' That's who'd inspired it after all.

'No not her. I don't mind a bit of Madonna. I like that song you know, the Virgin one. I'm thinking of Patrick's friend.' She had the lemony lips she always wore when Patrick's girlfriend Cindy was mentioned.

Moira couldn't quite make the connection herself but she put the bottle down. She'd had a better idea. Perhaps she could talk Mammy into buying a bottle of Allure. That way she could uses hers and she'd be able to splash out on the serum. It was smart thinking if she did say so herself.

Maureen however, had other ideas. 'I'm an Arpège woman, Moira, you know that. It's my signature fragrance so it is.'

'You're not Coco Chanel, Mammy.'

'Now listen to me, Moira O'Mara. If for some reason you found yourself in a dark room, lost and needing your mammy, would you or would you not be able to follow your sense of smell and find me?'

Moira shook her head slowly. On the one hand Mammy was right. She would indeed be able to sniff her out but on the other hand it was an out and out weird analogy to come up with. She sincerely hoped she'd never find herself in a darkened room trying to hunt her mammy down by smell alone.

Maureen O'Mara however had moved on and her eyes were darting around the dust free shelves. They were simply laden with gorgeous bottles yearning for a place on her dressing table but there was only one that would be given the honour. She spied the familiar stylish black and gold canister, by Lanvin. Classy, that's what it was, not like that pornographic thing Moira had been waving about. Maureen was an extremely loyal woman when it came to her scent. She harboured a secret fantasy that somehow Lanvin would get wind of this loyalty of hers and offer her a free lifetime supply of Arpège in exchange for her squirting it daily and spreading the joy. She picked up the bottle and stroked it lovingly for a beat before, ignoring the cardboard strips in the plastic container alongside it, she sprayed a heady cloud around her and closed her eyes to inhale the floral symphony.

Moira wafted her hand back and forth coughing. 'Jaysus, Mammy, I feel like I'm standing inside one of the glasshouses in the National Botanic Gardens.'

'Indeed, madam, Arpège is the fragrance of one thousand flowers,' cooed the consultant whose own eyes were watering with Maureen's heavy handedness. She'd seemingly materialised from thin air, lurking and ready to pounce from behind one of the shelves. A bony, hard-faced woman who was testing various lipsticks on the back of her hand nearby began to splutter and putting the tube back in the slot she flat-eyed Maureen. Moira didn't blame her. The odour wafting off her mammy was akin to walking into the toilet after the prior occupant had gone berserk with the air freshener. Still, it would take more than a lick of colour to soften that face she thought, defensively glaring back at her. It was like a blind cobbler's thumb.

'One thousand flowers you say?' Mammy squinted through the perfume atoms floating in the air to the consultant's badge. 'Eva. Now that's a pretty name so it is.' And just like that, she was away.

Moira smirked and left her bending Eva's ear while she went in search of her magical serum. She found it tucked in alongside a glorious selection of eternal youth potions and picked it up. The bottle was smooth and cool in her hand as the battle between the little common sense she had when it came to money and her conscience began.

'Moira, you are a woman in her mid-twenties do you really need an age-defying serum?'

'Yes I do. It's never too early to start planning for the future. I do believe the phrase is "future proofing". And, I like the bottle.'

'Sure, you pinched that from a building society advert, so you did.'

Moira sighed; it was true she had. Her conscience had played a blinder and she put the bottle down backing slowly away from it. It was time for a compromise and she made her mind up that if she had any credit left on her card at the end of the trip, she'd buy it on her return.

Eva, she noticed, approaching her and Mammy, was wearing a glazed smile that didn't quite stretch to the perfect liquid eyeliner flicks on either side of her eyes. She was, Moira guessed desperate to get a word in edgewise. Her chance came as Mammy was momentarily distracted by Moira's return. 'I hope you haven't been spending money you don't have.'

'I haven't.'

Eva jumped in. 'Madam we also have the fragrance in, erm,' she cleared her throat, 'Eau de Parfum. This stays on the skin longer and mellows throughout the day. Or, if Madam prefers, we have the concentrate perfume.' She eyed Maureen meaningfully. '*One* dab is all one needs.'

Moira had had enough; she wanted a cup of coffee and something to eat. She only had so much willpower and it was wavering. Time to put some distance between her and the serum. 'Don't encourage her,' she said to Eva. 'Would you want to sit next to one thousand flowers in a tin can with no windows? She'll be setting my hay fever off as it is.'

'Excuse my daughter, she forgot to pack her manners,' Maureen tutted. 'Thank you for your time, Eva. I won't be buying today because I have a bottle to tide me over on my holidays. Now then, did I tell you Moira and I are off to Vietnam?'

'Erm, you did, yes.' Eva looked like a mouse cornered by a cat and Moira felt a pang of sympathy. She'd been that mouse many times and as such she turned to her mammy and said, 'Mammy I just heard a lady over by the Elizabeth Arden stand saying she'd seen Daniel Day Lewis buying a slice of mud cake from Butler's Chocolate Café.' It was a total fib and Moira was normally a very truthful girl but desperate times called for desperate measures. Her rather enormous white lie would move Mammy over to where she wanted to be. Besides the chocolate café was a highlight of any trip to the airport and she wasn't about to miss out on a visit.

It worked a treat because at the mention of her favourite heartthrob, Mammy was off like a racehorse at the starter gate as the flag dropped. 'She loved him in Last of the Mohicans. It was the loin cloth that did it,' Moira said to an open-mouthed Eva, before following the trail of burning rubber, Mammy had left behind.

Chapter 5

'I know what you're going to say and it wasn't me,' Maureen shouted at her daughter. 'And don't interrupt me, I'm watching Entrapment. That Catherine Zeta Jones is very bendy, so she is. Sure you wouldn't believe the limbo dance she can do to get under those laser beam thing-a-me-bobs.' Maureen might have added that Moira had a look of Catherine about her but she didn't feel like giving her daughter a compliment. She still hadn't forgiven her for her little Daniel Day Lewis trick. It wasn't nice to get a woman all het up like that over nothing.

She turned her attention back to the screen in time to catch Sean Connery attempting some bending of his own. It didn't impress her; she'd never been a fan of his. Roger Moore was the Bond for her ever since she'd seen him in The Man with the Golden Gun. It was that film that had set this whole adventure in motion. The scene with Roger on the romantic old boat with its venetian blind-like sails had cemented a desire in her to one day sail on a junk. Preferably with Roger but Moira would have to do.

It had happened that one day she'd been out shopping for good quality walking shoes with her friend Rosemary—they belonged to the same rambling group—when she'd seen a poster of Ha Long Bay. She'd stood outside the Grafton Street Thomas Cook, mesmerised by the glossy photograph of limestone islands soaring out of emerald waters. That alone was breathtaking but it was the red-sailed junk that had captured her imagination and seen her drag Rosemary inside the travel agency.

Moira lifted the headphone away from Mammy's ear. 'Stop shouting,' she hissed. 'And it was so you. I told you not to eat the cheese.'

'It's not my fault. I think I may have a little intolerance problem.' She definitely wasn't going to say kind things to her daughter if she kept that up. Maureen folded her arms and tried to ignore her.

'Then why did you eat it? And such a great big wedge too.'

'Sure, what else was I supposed to have with the crackers?'

'You could have left them; nobody twisted your arm to eat them.'

'Moira, it was complimentary and the O'Mara family does not turn their nose up at complimentary.'

'Well I'm turning my nose up now, aren't I?' Moira let the headphone ping back against Mammy's ear and glanced past her to where the gentleman who'd told them he was in the importing and exporting business was asleep. He looked to be around his mid-fifties with a big head of badly dyed hair and the kind of girth that would make long haul flights uncomfortable. His importing and exporting, whatever that entailed, couldn't be doing that well, she thought, not if he couldn't stretch to a business class ticket.

He was late boarding and Moira was sure she'd caught a strong whiff of whisky coming off him as he'd squeezed into his seat muttering an apology. Once he'd managed to adjust his seatbelt he turned and offered up a brief greeting before, to Mammy's disappointment, putting his headphones on and closing his eyes. He hadn't so much as stirred since, not even when dinner was doing the rounds. Mammy was most concerned about him missing out on the beef noodle stir fry but Moira had managed to convince her that he wouldn't thank her for waking him.

She felt a stab of envy watching his chest heave with a contented snore. Oh, to be sound asleep like that. He must have taken something because while she was knackered, completely banjaxed in fact with her poor old body clock telling her it was way past her bedtime, she felt wired. There was too much going on around her and she shouldn't have had so many coffees. Lucky so and so she thought, screwing her nose up as she turned away, and not just because he had the aisle seat.

She normally loved the window seat but next to Mammy she felt trapped, squished in, and she twisted for the umpteenth time in her seat. She couldn't get comfortable and crossing then uncrossing her legs she mused that the lack of leg room was punishment for being economy passengers. Sure, it was torture the way you had to walk through business class when you boarded. Trying not to stare at them all spread out like they were on their sofas at home, blankets already tucked in around their laps. She'd been about to nod off an hour or so back when she'd been startled awake by a kick in the shin thanks to an unapologetic Mammy doing her ankle rotations. Now, she let out a huffy sigh and glanced at her watch. Jaysus, five more hours of this! It seemed an interminable amount of time and leaning her head back against the seat rest she closed her eyes and let her mind drift off.

Heathrow had been a nightmare; the busy hub was heaving due to a swirling fog that had plonked itself squarely over the London airport causing delays. She and Mammy had fought their way through the swarms of disgruntled travellers to collect their bags and had checked in with Thai Airways without drama. They'd been left with enough time for another cup of coffee, and to have a wander in order to stretch their legs before boarding their plane.

Moira was grateful for small mercies, like Mammy refraining from dousing herself in Arpège at the duty free this time round. She was sure she'd only gone without a free top up because of the little boy who'd had the misfortune to sit in front of them on their short British Airways hop. He'd announced in that loud and proud way of the under-fives that he reckoned Nana must be hiding on the plane because he could smell her stinky flower smell. Moira had elbowed Mammy but she'd pretended she hadn't heard.

Thanks to the fog, it was well over an hour before the plane that would take them on the last leg of their journey to Ho Chi Minh had been cleared for take-off. It was just long enough for her and Mammy to get edgy with one another. There they were trapped in their seats thinking about those feckers in business class as they sniped at one another—beholden to Mother Nature waving her wand and banishing the pea-souper. By gosh, at that moment in time, Moira would have loved a drink. Her mouth had watered at the thought of an icy cold glass of crisp, white wine.

She'd imagined the dry fruitiness smoothing out her ragged edges. Instead of imbibing she doused herself in Evian and as the pilot's voice finally crackled over the tannoy system, he'd come as a welcome distraction. The sound system was dodgy but she'd managed to string together enough of what he was announcing to know they were expecting to be airborne in the next half an hour or so. She'd sat digging her nails into her palms thinking unkind thoughts about the woman who'd birthed her sitting next to her.

Moira blinked, coming back to her present situation. Her eyes were dry from the air-conditioning; the Evian wouldn't do anything for that and she was beginning to feel a little cold. She retrieved the blanket from under the seat in front of her and ripped the plastic off before draping it over herself. Mammy she saw was still engrossed in her film. They'd stopped niggling at one another once dinner was served. All those foil sealed containers had broken the boredom as they'd peeled the lids back excited to see what was inside. Mammy had been most impressed with her meal as she said the last time she'd flown, a budget airline to Tenerife with Daddy, the meal had been so small 'it t'wuldn't fill the holes in yer teeth.' Moira jammed her pillow up against the window and leaned her head on it feeling the vibrating motion of the plane as she thought back on her going away dinner with Andrea.

They'd met at Zaytoon in Temple Bar for a chicken shish, too skint to stretch to anything fancier but both agreeing the Mediterranean food was to die for. Andrea had been trying to keep a straight face over her glass of Coke, the restaurant wasn't licensed which suited Moira just fine, at the thought of her friend backpacking around strange and exotic Far Eastern shores with her mammy.

'It's not funny.'

'Sure, you'd be falling about the place if the shoe were on the other foot.'

It was true she would have been. 'No I wouldn't, friends are supposed to support and sympathise with one another.'

Andrea had snorted. 'Ah well, on the bright side it's a good thing you're off for a bit because Friday night drinks are rolling around at the end of the week and someone is sure to shag someone they shouldn't. You and Michael will be old news by the time you get back.'

'But I didn't shag him.' Moira had defended herself.

'*I know that* but you can hardly make a public announcement to say that while you seriously entertained the idea of finding out what lay beneath that suit of his and taking him for a few laps around the race track you didn't actually pass the start line. And if he is after having extra marital affairs it's not with you.'

'He wasn't like that.'

'He was exactly like that Moira.'

Moira refused to believe *her* Michael, no scratch that he wasn't hers, never had been, made a habit of sleeping around on his wife. Andrea however had him pegged as a middle-aged cliché and would not be swayed from her way of thinking. It had been time to deflect the conversation away from herself. 'I wish you'd hurry up and give yer man one. That would give the Property girls something else to talk about. They're the worst so they are.'

'Conveyancing will do that to you, it's boring as shite. As for me and Connor, there's no chance. He's still dating the Amazonian Accountant.' Andrea had gotten that daft dreamy look at the thought of Connor Reid. It was the same expression she wore when she tucked into her bag of hot chips after a night on the lash.

'No, not Connor, you need to move on from that eejit. You do not want a man who fancies himself more than he fancies you, Andrea. Sure, you'd spend the rest of your days fighting for mirror space. I told you I caught him gazing at his reflection in the lift doors the other day. I'm talking about Jeremy from IT. He's cute in a computer man sort of a way.'

'I don't know why you seem so sure he fancies me.'

'Because of his exorbitant interest in your box that's why. He's forever after tinkering with it.'

Andrea's Coke had gone down the wrong way and as she coughed and spluttered, she sent tiny pieces of chopped lettuce flying off her plate. A couple glanced over alarmed, watching Moira get up to give her friend a few whacks on the back before fetching her a glass of water.

'Are you alright now?'

Andrea had nodded.

'I was talking about your computer by the way. You need to get your mind out of the gutter.'

The memory of that conversation made her smile but the smile faltered as an unpleasant smell wafted her way again. Mammy was shifting tellingly in her seat but had her eyes glued to the screen. Moira scowled at her even though she was oblivious. She felt bullied into this trip. It wasn't on her bucket list. She didn't have a bucket list for fecks sake, she was only in her twenties and as such never in a million trillion years had she thought she'd wind up where she was right now.

Ah she knew well enough it wasn't Mammy's fault she was here, not really. She'd gotten herself into a mess and Mammy was just trying to get her away from the pig's ear she'd made of her life for a while. That and fill Rosemary of the recent hip replacement's place. Why, oh, why couldn't Mammy have booked herself a lovely long holiday in Sydney where there were lots and lots of shops and beaches or, or, she cast around, Hawaii, she'd always fancied Hawaii. But no apparently, Mammy had a dream—a dream to sail on a fecking junk, and had decided that since you never knew what was waiting for you around the corner, the time had come to fulfil that dream.

Thinking about it, if anyone was to blame for her present predicament it was Mammy's so-called friend, Rosemary Farrell. It was her who'd left Mammy in the lurch. She'd decided she couldn't possibly go to Vietnam for a month with Maureen, not when Bold Breda was making eyes at the new fella in their rambling group. This was despite already having booked. She didn't want those bionic hips of hers going to waste. She hadn't actually said that last bit and Moira pushed the thought of Rosemary getting up to shenanigans aside only to find the space instantly filled by Michael Daniel's handsome face. She felt the familiar pang as she conjured up those beautiful eyes of his. Eyes she'd lost herself in. What there'd been between them had ended before it really began which was a blessing because she was not the sort of girl to have a fling with a married man. Although, she'd come close, too close for comfort.

In that respect it would be good to put some distance between herself and Michael because it was hard seeing him at work. There was part of her that longed for a glimpse of him, while the other half found it crushingly painful when she did catch sight of him. She'd never been the sort of girl to get red in the face and flustered when it came to men either but each time she set eyes on him she turned into a gibbering, scarlet faced imbecile. It wasn't professional and people had noticed. She didn't much like being the subject of office gossip and felt guilty for the times she'd gleefully listened to a juicy morsel being whispered over the top of the reception desk before repeating it to Andrea over lunch.

As for Michael he was seemingly unaffected by her presence and unfailingly polite when he spoke to her, which was only when strictly necessary. The consummate professional with his head held high around the law offices where he was a partner in the Aviation and Asset Finance department. The tattle about him and Moira was circulating like a virus travelling through the air conditioning ducts but it didn't seem to touch him. Whereas her face ignited every time she walked into the tea room and the conversation came to a halt. Her sudden sabbatical would only add fuel to the fire but it would soon sputter away to nothing when she wasn't sitting at her reception-desk post serving as a reminder to those with nothing better to talk about.

She thumped the pillow. Perhaps if she put some classical music on it might clear her racing thoughts and soothe her off to sleep. She dug out the headphones and plugged them in before fiddling with the remote until she found something suitable.

Chapter 6

M aureen watched the credits roll down on the small screen in front of her. It hadn't been a bad sort of a film even if Roger wasn't in it. It had served its purpose and successfully whiled away a couple of hours. The man next to her was still sound asleep and taking off her headphones she could hear his raspy snores. Moira she saw had dropped off too. She'd always looked like she was catching flies when she was asleep, she thought with a fond smile as she caught sight of her daughter's open mouth. The poor love was exhausted, she always got snarky when she was tired—had done since she was a baby. She was the same when she was hungry.

The poor love had been a lost soul since her daddy had died, Maureen thought, feeling the pangs of maternal guilt at not having been there for her youngest daughter. Her bottom lip quivered and she resisted the urge to reach out and stroke her dark hair. She'd been an ostrich where Moira was concerned. She knew she'd developed a strong liking for the sauce. The girl was greener around the gills each time she saw her than a frog, and she should have put her foot down long before she'd gotten herself involved with *that* man. Sure, she'd been a neglectful Mammy but, she'd prayed hard and look what had happened. They'd been given a chance to reconnect. Maureen yawned, she was bone tired too but she'd never been one for sleeping on planes or in cars, or anywhere for that matter, unless she was lying horizontal. She'd just have to catch up when they got to their hotel.

She caught sight of the presentable young woman with her hair slicked back in a glossy bun making her way down the aisle with her trolley. How did the cabin crew all manage to look so groomed? The girl didn't have so much as a hair out of place and her make-up was perfect whereas she felt like a crumpled auld wreck. Reaching Maureen's row, she offered her a glass of water with a beatific smile which she accepted gratefully. It dehydrated you flying so it did and she'd never understood people who filled themselves with drink like Mr Whisky-a-go-go next to her. She could get tipsy off the smell of him alone.

Maureen nursed her water as the trolley rattled off and marvelled over the fact she was on her way. Who'd have believed it? She, Maureen O'Mara, the girl from Ballyclegg, was over half way to Vietnam! When she was young just going to the capital constituted an overseas trip. Ah well now, maybe that was a bit of an exaggeration but it wasn't all that much of a stretch. She wondered what her mam and da would make of what she was up to if they were still alive. They'd never approved of much when it came to their only daughter, and they'd probably think she was mad, just like they had when she'd run off all those years ago. Life had a funny way of working out though because if she hadn't of gotten on that bus to Dublin, she'd never have met her Brian.

At the thought of her husband her eyes burned and she bit down on her bottom lip to stop the tears from spilling over. She was prone to being tearful but she didn't cry over Brian in public. That was her cardinal rule and she'd not broken it, not once in the two years since he'd passed. She could cry over waving goodbye to her daughter for a month, or a scene from Ballykissangel—mind, Sunday evening's episode had had her wanting to bang that Assumpta Fitzgerald and Father Peter's heads together. Sure, the sexual tension between the pair of them would have you on the edge of your seat shouting at the television for them to just get on with it. Other weeks watching the show, she'd cry buckets. When it came to Brian though, well those great big ugly sobs that would rack forth at the thought of however many years she had left without him, well now they were best left for when her front door was firmly shut.

People said time healed. This was true on some levels because Maureen knew by the tight fit of her clothes that she no longer wore the signs of grief physically. One's appetite could only disappear for so long! Emotionally however it was a different matter. Some folk dealt with grief by wallowing while others were stoic, choosing to soldier on. Maureen had always had to fight for what she wanted in life and she was no wallower.

Instead of retreating inside herself like a snail into its shell which is exactly what she'd wanted to do, she'd launched into action by announcing she was moving out of the family home. She hoped to leave the daily reminders that Brian was no longer by her side, sharing the load and decision making when it came to the day to day running of O'Mara's, and make a fresh start by the sea.

So, she'd bought an apartment, not a flat because apartment had a much more sophisticated ring to it, in Howth. She'd gadded about, joining every committee and social group for retirees on offer, with the energy of a girl half her age.

Thanks-be-to-God, Aisling had refused to let her sell the guesthouse and had taken over its running; a grand job she was making of it too. To offload the old girl as she thought of O'Mara's would have been a decision made in haste, and one she knew now she'd have lived to regret.

O'Mara's was a family business and it was important it stayed in the family. Had she sold the resplendent Georgian home, Brian would have surely turned in his grave. Not everybody had been happy with Aisling's decision though; Patrick had huffed off to America. It had hurt Maureen to think her oldest child, and only son had no interest in carrying on the business despite her protestations that the O'Mara children had the right to follow their own dreams and not step into those that had belonged to their parents.

Patrick had wanted his share of the cash from the business so he could invest it in whatever scheme he was involved with over there in La La Land as she thought of Los Angeles. Sure it wasn't where his real life was and look at the state of his lady friend, Cindy, or was it Cynthia, and that enormous bosom of hers? What woman in her right mind would pay good money to stand in the shower and not be able to see their toes? Sure, that came around soon enough as it was. She cast a baleful glance at her midriff. Moira was right; she shouldn't have eaten the cheese she was awfully bloated as a result. Cynthia or Cindy was a woman who clearly wore her brains in her bosom, Maureen had her number.

Patrick was a good boy but he clearly had his brains somewhere else too when it came to his girlfriend. He was all about the money was Pat. He hadn't always been like that but these last few years he'd become like a shark. Money, he would learn, could you buy a lot of things but it couldn't buy you the love of a good woman and a happy life. Still in all it was no good her telling him that, he'd learn the hard way. You had to step back where your children were concerned, like she'd done in the end with Roisin. She wasn't one for meddling, well not much anyway.

Maureen sighed, you never stopped worrying about your children from the moment they came kicking and bawling into the world. No matter if they were two years old or pushing forty, you still worried and it had been easier to bear the weight of that worry when she'd had Brian to share it with.

His passing had changed them all. Her life had been tootling along nicely, their children were all grown, they ran a successful guesthouse, and they were as much in love with one another as they had been from the moment they'd met. Then Brian got sick. It hadn't been part of their plan and she'd refused to face it for the longest time, refused to accept her big strong Brian wouldn't be there for her, until he began to wither before her very eyes.

The fall-out from his illness was plain to see where their children were concerned too. Poor Moira had bounced from mistake to mistake. Aisling had gone and gotten engaged to that eejit but at least she'd seen sense and was with lovely Quinn now. Maureen had high hopes of welcoming Quinn into the family fold before too long and she smiled at the thought of it. Rosi was the one who'd probably coped the best out of all them, removed as she had been from the daily indignity of illness by distance. Besides, she couldn't fall apart, not with Colin and little Noah to look after.

The thought of her grandson warmed her. She'd promised to send him a postcard from every place they visited on their travels. He loved getting mail. She could picture him abandoning his breakfast to run to the front door as he heard the mail get pushed through the slot. As for Pat, well he'd decided the grass was greener in Los Angeles. A silly analogy because the grass was most definitely not greener. There was nowhere in the world with grass as green as Ireland as Brian used to say each spring when St Stephen's Green came back to life.

She winced, half expecting to taste blood where she'd bitten her lip this time. *Mustn't cry, mustn't cry.* She couldn't very well do what she normally did which was keep herself busy. She was stuck in this seat for the next few hours. At home she had her rambling group, her art classes, and sailing lessons to while away the days. The thing was, none of those things filled her long, lonely evenings. There were times she'd be sitting in her living room on her new sofa in her new apartment and if she stared at the four walls around her long enough, she could conjure Brian up. All of a sudden, he'd be there standing in front of her, so real she'd reach out to trace her finger down the lines and crevices of time etched on his beloved face but her finger would slice through the air. She'd blink and the image before her would disperse like tiny granules of coloured sand running through her fingers. She'd never breathed a word of that to anyone; they'd think she was mad but that's when she'd let herself cry those ugly sobs.

Ah, Brian. What would he think of her and Moira winging their way to Vietnam? They'd had grand plans of travelling the world together when they retired. Mind they'd always thought

Patrick would be the one to take over O'Mara's when that day came. They'd been wrong about so many things. They'd kept a list, her and Brian, of places they'd visit one day. They'd had a curiosity about the world outside their guesthouse, which perhaps was due to their guests. They'd met so many interesting people from so many different places over the years. They'd both loved nothing more than to listen to the stories their visitors had to tell about the places they called home. Vietnam hadn't been on that list and Maureen suspected that's why it had held such appeal. It was somewhere different, somewhere she might just be able to stop and breathe. She wasn't a proponent of what she called Oprah phrases—words like journey and the such irked her, but in this case, she'd make an allowance because that was exactly what she was embarking on. A journey to try and reconnect with who she, Maureen O'Mara, was without Brian.

As she drained her cup, she realised she needed the toilet. It wasn't good for a woman who'd borne four children to hold on she thought eying the snoring lump next to her. What were her chances of waking him, she wondered? She gave him a tentative tap on the arm, 'Excuse me,' she said and then again in a louder voice with a much firmer tap but to no avail. He didn't move so much as a muscle. Maureen pursed her lips; it was no good. She couldn't hang around waiting for him to come out of his alcohol induced slumber. There was nothing for it, she'd have to go over him.

She unbuckled and got out of her seat, turning around in the cramped space so she was holding the back of her seat. The man in the seat behind her gave her a weary smile, before tuning back into his screen. The passengers either side of him were asleep—the woman on his left resting her head on his shoulder. It was now or never she thought attempting to swing a leg over Mr Whisky-a-go-go. He was a big man and she was a little woman. Her leg wouldn't quite stretch to the aisle floor, not unless she propelled herself nimbly over, like a sideways attempt at the vault. She'd been good at gym as a child. Sister Abigail had said she plenty of spring in her. *On the count of three, Maureen*, she could almost hear Sister Abigail's voice as she counted, 'One, two, and three, up and over.' Only this time she didn't quite make it across, landing instead in an undignified heap spread-eagled on Mr Whisky-a-go-go's lap, her bosom pressed firmly against his lolling head. That was when she heard a voice.

'Mammy, what the feck are you doing?!'

Chapter 7

'For the tenth time, Moira I was not straddling him!' Maureen's eyes never moved from the carousel. They were in the arrivals hall of Tan Son Nhat Airport. There was only one bag left winding its way around on the belt in front of them and it wasn't hers. The black shiny case shuddered past once more teasing her as Moira, who was leaning against the trolley upon which she'd heaved her pack, refused to let the incident on Flight TG485 go.

'I saw you with my own two eyes, Mammy, and it did not look good. They have laws about that sort of thing on aeroplanes you know.' Okay, she was taking things a bit far but it had been a long flight and the drama that had unfolded as Mr Whisky-a-go-go nearly choked in Mammy's cleavage had been too much for her fuddled brain to take.

'Jesus wept, Moira, that's the mile-high club so it is and all I was doing was trying to get to the toilet for a wee! Was it my fault the drunken eejit wouldn't wake up?' Maureen's patience too was wearing thin and her voice had gone up several octaves. She'd had enough.

'Shush would you.' Moira furtively glanced around her. 'Everyone and their mammy doesn't need to know your business.' Actually the crowds had thinned out considerably and she wasn't fancying Mammy's chances where her bag was concerned. It had been a good five minutes since the last of their fellow passengers had retrieved their bag from the carousel and gone on their way. She supposed they should go and find someone to tell.

FORTY-FIVE MINUTES later, minus one bag but with assurances from a most apologetic Thai Airways that it would be delivered to their hotel sometime tomorrow, a disgruntled Maureen followed Moira's lead. They were following the signs to the exit that would take them to the taxi rank. The helpful woman on the Tourist Information desk had booked them into a very reasonable hotel for the night, before gesturing in the direction of the exit where they would find the metered taxis. One thing mother and daughter had whole heartedly agreed on was that neither was up for hostels. There would be no dormitories, six to a room, drunken bunkmates on this trip. Two to a room was going to be struggle enough, thank you very much.

Maureen spied the Foreign Exchange desk and subconsciously rested her hand on her bum bag where their funds were tucked safely away. They had enough money to tide them over in the meantime. She'd organised it through the AIB at home and had both Vietnamese dong and US dollars. She was more partial to the dong because her couple of hundred punt had officially made her a millionaire in Vietnam.

The name of their hotel was, Dong Do and their Tourist Information lady had neatly printed it for them on the piece of paper Moira, not trusting Mammy and her pants of many pockets, had put in her pants of only two pockets. She pushed her trolley through the sliding doors to the waiting night outside and gasped as the heat and hordes of shouting people descended on them. Sweatpants and joggers were a mistake she thought, because it was like someone had thrown an electric blanket over the top of her and hundreds of strangers had decided to crawl underneath it with her. She felt momentarily panicked by the foreign scene and her last coherent thought before Mammy took charge was this humidity would be murder on her hair; she was justified in packing her hair straighteners.

Mammy was magnificent, a warrior woman, Moira admiringly pushed the trolley after her as she blazed a trail through the hotel touts with their flapping brochures to the white airport taxi at the front of the line. The little man got out of his car and with a superhuman strength hauled her pack into his boot, while someone, Moira never saw who whisked the trolley away. She and Mammy collapsed into the back seat of the cab shutting the doors on the chaos outside. The air-conditioned calm was blissful and they sighed their relief simultaneously. Their driver got behind the wheel and Moira passed him the paper with the name of the hotel. He nodded and Mammy watched hawkeyed to see he set his metre before deftly weaving his way out of the busy hub.

A few minutes later Moira and Mammy had exhausted polite conversation with their driver. His English was limited and Moira was too tired to pick out phrases from the guide book. As for Mammy, well she was still sulking over her errant pack. Both women peered out their respective windows as they moved away from the airport and out onto the main road. Their eyes widened at the cacophonous horns mingling with shouts but it was the sights swarming around the vehicle that made their jaws drop. On either side of them a veritable ocean of mopeds and motorcycles whizzed around, behind, and in front of them.

'Mammy, look.' Moira stabbed at the glass, her exhaustion momentarily replaced by wonder. 'There were four on that bike, two little ones and their mammy and daddy. None of them had helmets on either.'

Maureen peered around her daughter, watching in amazement as families went about their business. Youngsters were indeed sandwiched between their parents on mopeds. Their small faces taking what, to the uninitiated, seemed like mayhem in their stride, some were even sleeping. Teens flirted with one another in an age-old ritual only instead of sidling alongside one another at the dance as they had in her day, they rode alongside one another on their mopeds. Pretty girls two to a scooter with flowing black hair smiling back at grinning lads determined to keep pace. 'Mother of God it's like watching Blind Date on scooters,' she muttered. Her eyes caught those of their driver who was watching their reaction to the scenes around them with amusement.

'Only without Cilla,' Moira echoed.

Maureen didn't know she'd been holding her breath until they pulled up outside a respectable looking hotel on a leafy street. Their driver deserved a medal in her opinion for dealing with those roads, he must have nerves of steel because hers were shredded. 'Dong Do,' he grinned over his shoulder before getting out and opening Moira's door. The taxi drivers back home could learn a thing or two about customer service, Maureen thought sliding across the seat to exit.

The heat after the cool of the car came as a shock and she stood on the cracked old pavement blinking in wonderment at the busy, neon-lit scene around them. Their driver retrieved Moira's bag from the boot and bent double, staggered with it toward the hotel. Moira scurried after him and Maureen watched as a smartly dressed night porter opened the door and relieved him of it, placing it on a trolley.

She was reluctant to head inside just yet and a frisson of excitement penetrated Maureen's jet lagged torpor, tomorrow she'd get to explore this place. She could already see it was like nowhere she'd ever been in her life. A horn blared and a pair of young men roared past on their Hondas making her jump. She realised the porter was holding the door waiting for her and so smiling her thanks at him she went inside.

'Make sure you tip him well, Mammy,' Moira whispered nodding at their patient driver before making for the smiling receptionist. She wondered whether this young woman kept a stash of biscuits in her top drawer like their receptionist, Bronagh. Did Vietnamese people even eat biscuits? She hadn't a clue. The only thing she was certain was a national staple was rice.

Maureen made the driver blush as she flashed her midriff once more attempting to find the right notes, stashed inside her bum bag. He'd set his price in American dollars and at this moment in time she was grateful as it was easier to fish out two five-dollar notes, she was tipping him generously, than to sort her thick wad of Vietnamese dong. He seemed pleased with the tip and there were lots of nods and smiles and little bows on both their parts until Moira having had enough called her over.

'Mammy, c'mon, we need to check in.'

MAUREEN DIDN'T ASK for a lot when it came to her accommodation but it wasn't too much to ask for a soft bed, hot water and a flushing loo. Oh, and cleanliness was next to godliness in her book. You should be able to run a finger down the skirting board and have it come up clean, so you should. This was a test she'd often employed at O'Mara's and not once, in all her years of running the old place had anyone ever complained that their room was not up to standard. Sure, a clean room wasn't too much to ask when you were paying good money to stay in an establishment now was it?

So no, she wasn't a woman of fancy tastes. She'd never had champagne tastes on beer money—mind she wasn't sure about Moira. She cast a cursory glance in her daughter's direction as they rode the lift to the third floor in silence. Moira seemed to subscribe to the theory that it was better to spend money like there was no tomorrow than to spend tonight like there's no money. Maureen's lips tightened; she was a spendthrift that girl of hers. She shook her head as the lift groaned ominously. It was down to that ridiculously overstuffed pack. If they wound up stuck in the elevator for the night it would be her five pairs of shoes, fifteen outfit changes and God only knew what else that would be to blame.

This line of thought made her think of her own missing backpack and that made her frown but she was distracted from dwelling on it by the lift juddering to a halt and the doors sliding open—thanks be to God. The porter trundled off down the tiled corridor, the wheels of the trolley echoing loudly in the silence as the two women dutifully followed. He stopped outside room 310 and unlocked the door, wheeling Moira's pack inside and lifting it onto the luggage rack before standing to one side to let Moira and Maureen see their room.

Maureen clapped her hands in delight. It was very, well, exotic Far East. The décor was a montage of rich reds and dark, ornately carved wood. It was the polar opposite of O'Mara's with its Georgian grandeur and it was perfect. She caught Moira's eye and remembered to tip their porter before going through the smiling, nodding, bowing process once more until as if they were playing rock-paper-scissors, he conceded and left them to it, closing the door behind him. Outside they could hear the faint sound of the horns and rumbling roar of motorbike engines. A fluorescent glow emanated from signage across the road. Maureen moved over to the window and closed the blinds shutting the foreign world below them out. It could wait until tomorrow.

'We made it,' Moira announced, flopping down on the bed closest the door. 'Bags first shower.'

'Five minutes and no longer, Moira. I'm shattered so I am, I want to get to bed.' Maureen watched her daughter as she got up and moved toward her pack. A minute or so later as she'd finally located her toilet bag and pyjamas she muttered, 'I could have been in and out of the shower in the time it took you to find those.'

'They were right down the bottom.' Moira marched into the bathroom and closed the door firmly behind her. She eyed the dish by the sink with its array of tiny tubes and bottles, tempted to inspect them all but thought better of it. Instead, she turned the handle on the shower around to hot and stepping under the jets had a quick wash. She felt one hundred times better by the time she reappeared in the bedroom. A flannel, soap, and hot water was a marvellous thing she thought, retrieving an oversized T-shirt from her pack and tossing it at Mammy. 'There you go, you can sleep in that tonight.'

Ten minutes later the luxury of stretching out in bed was wearing thin, Moira wanted to turn the light out. Her body was crying out for sleep but Mammy was still faffing around in the bathroom. 'What are you doing in there?'

'I'm just drying myself off. I had to wash my knickers so I've a pair for the morning.'

'Sure you can borrow a pair from me. I've plenty. Just hurry up would ya, I'm knackered.'

'I will not wear a pair of those wisps of string you call knickers.'

'G-string, Mammy and they stop VPL.'

'I don't want to know what VPL is when it's at home, sure it sounds like some terrible disease down yonder.' The door opened and Mammy appeared in a T-shirt that came down to the middle of her thighs, her chest was emblazoned in red with the words 'Red Hot Chili Peppers – One Hot Minute Tour 95. Her face was shiny, scrubbed clean.

Moira's eyes narrowed. 'You used my Elizabeth Arden exfoliating cleanser, didn't you?'

'No.' Maureen fibbed. She had and her skin felt marvellous.

Moira wasn't convinced. Mammy better not have used her toothbrush or there'd be trouble she thought, but she was too tired to pursue it further. 'Hurry up and put the light out.' She curled up pulling the sheets up under her chin. The air-conditioning was keeping the room at an almost chilly level but she suspected if they turned it off the room would soon be stiflingly, stuffy.

Maureen pulled back the red coverlet and clambered into bed. The mattress was firmer than she was used to but sure, it would be good for her poor auld back. The sheets however were crisp, cool and fresh smelling as if they'd spent the day snapping in the breeze, just the way she liked them. Although, if they had been snapping on the breeze outside, she suspected they'd smell more of petrol fumes than the clean starched smell of laundry currently pleasing her nostrils. She reached up and flicked the light off.

'G'night, Mammy.'

'G'night, Moira, love.'

Chapter 8

Mammy's Travel Journal

Hello from Ho Chi Minh! What an eye opener our first day's been. It's just after five o'clock and mine and Moira's feet are in bits from all the walking we did this morning. You wouldn't believe the things we've seen but I'm getting ahead of myself. I'll start at the beginning.

We slept for ten hours solid. I'll admit to feeling a bit like the back end of a bus when I woke up and yes, I used Moira's mascara even though she says sharing eye make-up will give you the pink eye but what she doesn't know won't hurt her. Sure, as it was, I had to put up with itching eyes all day and kept rubbing at them. By the time we got back to the hotel I looked like yer man Alice Cooper. I learned my lesson. I do like that exfoliating scrub of hers though.

The restaurant where we could get breakfast, it's included and is very good value, is on the top floor of our hotel. We had a grand view over the Saigon River and we sat watching all the activity on the streets below. I was a bit worried as to what would be on offer but we ate very normal breakfasty things, you know eggs, toast and the like but, the gentleman at the table in front of ours was slurping up some sorta broth. It had big, fat white noodles in it that reminded me of worms. Honestly, it was like that old Jerry Lewis recording of The Noisy Eater and him in a suit too. Moira said it was making her feel sick which I thought was a bit pot calling the kettle black. You'd want to have heard the racket she used to make sucking her spaghetti noodles up when it was Monday night, Spag Bog. I told her this and it didn't go down well.

I think I was feeling outa sorts because I'd slept heavy and because of my missing backpack. It's not a nice feeling knowing your smalls and other personal items are in the hands of strangers. I felt much better once I'd had a cup of coffee and as we walked back to our room, I resolved to be nice. No more sniping. God works in mysterious ways you know because not two minutes after we'd shut the door behind us there was a knock. I opened it, to be greeted by a different but equally noddy, smiley porter as the one we encountered last night and, he had my backpack on his trolley! I could of kissed him.

I didn't of course but I did send up a quick prayer of thanks and, of course I tipped him generously. I felt a little bad because even though I was eternally grateful to him for returning my bag to me, I had to shut the door on him in the end. He wasn't playing the rock-paper-scissors game like the other fella had and we'd have been there all day with the smiling and nodding.

I don't mind telling you it was a load off my mind to have my luggage and the first thing I did was put on a fresh bra and change my top. I treated myself to a blue one and a green one in the quick drying fabric. They were pricey like but to my mind well worth every penny. I put the blue one on and washed the green one I'd worn on the plane in the bathroom sink. I hung it over the shower rail and would you believe it? It's bone dry now. Sure, it's marvellous stuff. Moira says they might be quick drying but they're a fashion affront. I ignored her, because I'm being nice.

Anyway we decided we'd explore the sights on foot. Although Moira quite liked the look of those cyclo thing-a-me-bobs. They're a sorta three wheeled bicycle taxi but I told her no. I'd feel awful sitting there like Lady Muck, so I would, while yer poor wee man pedalled away looking like he was about to expire at any minute.

Stepping outside the hotel was like wading into warm soup and there were even more motorbikes zooming the streets than there'd been the night before. They're a menace so they are. Moira and I agreed there must be at least a million of the things buzzing about the place and from what we could see there are no road rules. It's a case of survival of the fittest.

Moira was in charge of the guidebook because she has a better sense of direction than I do and I've never been any good at reading the maps. Brian used to say road signs were like a foreign language to me. So, Moira took the lead and we set off admiring the grand old buildings. They reminded me of a film I once saw. It was set around a big white hotel in Singapore. I remember a fan rotating lazily around and people lounging about in cane chairs sipping cocktails. It might have been a Bond one if there were cocktails involved but I can't remember for certain.

In between these smart buildings there were tall, narrow shops with shuttered windows. There was lots of silk for sale too, jewel bright fabrics decorating the shop windows, and it was like a magnet pulling me and Moira in through the door so as we could stroke and admire them. I bought a pashmina for myself and each of my girls, excluding Moira because she's getting the trip and the other two aren't. Moira bought herself a pretty black sleeveless top with a band of red silk around the hemline. We had to remind ourselves it was the first day of our holiday and not to go mad with the spending.

The noise is like nothing else, the constant sounding of horns, shouts and construction work which is going on everywhere. It wasn't long before we happened across Notre Dame Cathedral, not the Paris one obviously. This Notre Dame was built with red bricks and had twin spires. I felt right at home when I set eyes on it the way I always do when I see God's House. Moira says she feels like that when she sees the McDonald's big yellow arches. They comfort her because she knows there's food, drink, and a toilet close at hand. The women trickling in and out of the cathedral clutching their rosary beads were wearing silk tunics in all the colours of a bird of paradise, and black pants, not at all the sort of getup you'd see back home. Moira and I lit a candle and I said a prayer. I'm not telling you who I prayed for though, that's private.

Outside the cathedral there were lots of men shouting at us 'would we like a ride in their cyclo?' No we would not. There were groups of children vying for our attention too, they were selling postcards. There was one little lad whose smile reminded me of Noah's, he looked to be around the same age as him too. Imagine, five years old and already out contributing to the family coffers. I'll have to tell Rosi. She can't even get Noah to put his pyjama pants under his pillow of a morning. I wanted to buy cards off all of them but Moira pulled me away after I'd bought my tenth.

We were grand, Moira and I, as we carried on with our exploring until we came to the intersection we needed to cross in order to visit the Ben Than market. There was no nice green man to bleep and let everybody know it was our turn to cross the road and so we stood by the kerb watching all those millions of scooters pass by like a pair of lemons. Of course the longer we stood there the more frightened of stepping out into all that chaos we became. Then would you believe it? A little old lady happened upon us.

She spoke to us but of course we couldn't understand a word, and she couldn't understand a word we were saying but you know sometimes you don't need language to communicate. She gave us a big toothless grin, took us both by the arm and steered us out into the traffic. Well now let me tell you, she was like Moses parting the Red Sea. She trotted across that road dragging us along with her, and every single one of those scooters whose path we were stepping into weaved their way around us.

We did the noddy, smiley thing once we'd made it to the other side and then we went our separate ways. The market was undercover and very hot and cramped. It had all sorts of things in it from teeny tiny shoes to teeny tiny tea sets. We were fascinated by the fish market at the far end. Every kind of fish was flapping around and the crabs, well, you'd want to see the size of the pincers on them. If one of them got hold of your toe at the beach you'd know about it. There were even rogue frogs making a bid for freedom. I suppose the frogs is down to the French influence on the place.

We had a sit down once we'd had a good look around. It was time for a cool drink along with a cheese baguette, lovely and light the bread was too with a crispy crust. Nature called after that.

It was no easy feat to find a public convenience because Moira couldn't find the word for toilet in our guide book. In the end I did a knock-kneed demonstration and we got pointed in the right direction. Like I said sometimes you can communicate without language. It was one of them squat toilets and we had to pay a lady for a piece of toilet paper. I was dubious as to whether I'd get back up again and I was terrified I'd lose my footing and slip or something, but sure I was grand. It's a blessing Rosemary didn't come with me because she's been making noises about her knees giving her trouble. Moira whose knees are perfectly fine made an almighty fuss about the cleanliness of the facility and I told her to cop on to herself. Sometimes that girl doesn't know she's born. Sure when I was a girl, we had an outhouse down the bottom of the yard. It was dark and full of spiders with hairy legs just waiting to get you.

I think Moira was tetchy because she was in pain. She said she'd had enough walking and asked me if I'd brought the Lanacane gel with me. I said no but I did have hand sanitizer. Well she ate the head off me. I told her not to take that tone with me and that if she'd worn the elephant pants her sister had given her instead of a silly short skirt, she'd be grand. She still says she won't be seen dead in the elephant pants and I said that she's not to come crying to me when she's red raw. I don't know where that one gets her stubborn streak from.

As it happened, I'd had enough of the walking too so we caught a taxi to the tourist office because we needed to buy our tickets for the hop on, hop off bus we're going to take to Hanoi. Would you believe our ticket only cost twenty-eight American dollars each? I tell you Bus Eireann are running a racket. I think I might have to write a letter to the man in charge when I get home. We're being robbed so we are. We've also booked a day trip tomorrow to the Mekong Delta, $14.00 with lunch, inclusive. Now, if that's not good value I don't know what is.

We visited the War Remnants Museum next. It was very upsetting so it was and I don't really want to talk about it. All I will say is there are never any winners in war not when you're a Mammy. I did have my photograph taken by a fighter plane though, and Moira posed by a US helicopter.

My observations from today are that this country has come through a terrible time and despite hardship the people are lovely. They're ever so smiley and noddy and always keen to help you. It gives you faith in the human spirit. Oh, and I like the Buddhist monks too, they have a gentle manner about them, not at all fierce like Father John can be if you miss the mass. And I think their robes are very sensible given the hot weather.

Postcard

DEAR NOAH,

It's your nana here. Aunty Moira and I have been having a grand time in Hoi Chi Minh or Saigon which is what the people who live here call it. It's very confusing, so it is. It's a big, busy city even busier than yer man Richard Scarry's Busytown in those books of his you love. I've never seen so many motorcycles in my life. There are thousands of them on the roads. There's lots to see here and it's a very interesting city. The sounds and the smells are very different to home. It's also the hottest place I've ever been. Noah, I hope you're being a good boy for your mammy and dad give them a hug from me and have one for yourself.

Love Nana

Chapter 9

Sally-Ann

Sally-Ann Jessop inhaled sharply, it couldn't be, could it? Surely it was too much of a coincidence that she should smell that particular smell, here, now. She'd definitely caught a strong whiff of that soft flowery scent she'd once adored though. It had made her look up sharply from her guidebook and she was certain it was the dark-haired woman who was wearing it. She looked to be around her age, only with skin that hadn't baked under a hot, unforgiving Australian sun. She was making her way in a bustling manner down the narrow aisle, a younger woman—she had to be her daughter—was following behind her.

The daughter appeared to be having a spot of difficulty, Sally-Ann noticed, the nurse in her concerned to see she was walking quite bow-legged. The poor girl had a nasty eye infection taking hold too, she hoped she had some antibiotic drops for it. Despite the puffy eye she couldn't help but notice she was lovely looking. She reminded Sally-Ann of an American actress, and she wracked her brain for the woman's name *Dee Dee or Dina,* but it wouldn't come to her. She was identical to her mother, the Arpège wearer, just younger.

Sally-Ann would know that fragrance anywhere although she hadn't worn the scent herself in well over thirty years. Not since she'd last set foot on Vietnamese soil. It held too many memories. Smells were a powerful tool for triggering the memory she'd learned. They were every bit as powerful as sounds. Even now, all these years later a sudden bang like the back firing of a car or a tardy Guy Fawkes cracker would send her diving for cover but the smell of Arpège, well that took her right back in time to what was another world now.

It never left you, the fear and the instinct to survive. Poor Robert had suffered terribly with nightmares for the rest of his life once he'd returned home. He'd cry out in his sleep and she'd know he was reliving things no young man should ever have to live through. Her breath caught in her throat as she thought of her husband, and the familiar lump that warned her that tears weren't far away formed. She swallowed hard and took a few steadying breaths becoming aware that the two women, a few seats behind her now, were bickering, and eager for distraction she tuned in.

'Mammy, I get the window seat. Sure, it's only fair.'

'Why? You had the window seat on the plane and it's not my fault you've got the pink eye.'

'That was no picnic, squashed into the corner I was for thirteen hours. And it is your fault. I know you used my mascara.'

'I wouldn't do that, Moira, but sure, I haven't even had a cup of coffee yet and the sun's only just after rising. It's too early for arguing. Take the window seat, and I want to hear no more about it.'

'Aha, I knew it. You do feel guilty.'

Sally-Ann's mouth twitched as, glancing over her shoulder, she was in time to see the younger woman wag a finger at her mother before sliding into the seat. She wasn't going to give her a chance to change her mind.

She'd always been one of life's people watchers, happy to sit back and listen and tuning in now she liked the sing-song quality of their Irish accents. To her ears the Irish always sounded like they were telling a story even when they were just wrangling over who sat where. You couldn't say that about the Australian accent with its lazy, drawling vowels. She knew it sounded brutal and harsh to delicate ears but then you had to be both of those to survive the conditions in the dusty old sheep farm she'd always called home.

She admired their dark Celtic looks too, they were both dainty, petite women. It was a category the feminine kernels beneath her sun-worn exterior had always yearned to fit into. Ha, she thought to herself glancing down at the age spots decorating the back of her hands, thanks to that damned sun, there'd never been any chance of that. She'd tipped six foot by the time she was sixteen and had filled out into the sort of solid build that had people describe her as a strong Sheila. A strong Sheila was not something she'd wanted to be at sweet sixteen but it had served her well over the years because if she hadn't of been strong, inside and out, she wouldn't have survived. Yes, these hands of hers might be worn and coarse to touch, the hands of a worker, but they were also healing hands. She was proud of them.

The mother flopped down into her seat and looking up caught Sally-Ann watching them. She smiled and shrugged in that universal way women do when it comes to their offspring. Sally-Ann smiled back. She'd been there done that with her own kids. Jeff and Teagan were both off living their own lives now though and she could imagine their faces if she'd suggested they make this a mother, daughter, son trip to Vietnam! She was intrigued as to why these two were travelling together. It wasn't the norm, she thought, her attention flickering to the front of the bus. A young woman with matted hair on the verge of forming dreadlocks had just boarded. She was cutting it fine Sally-Ann thought, watching as puffing and panting she showed the driver her ticket.

Jeff and Teagan had both been uncertain about her heading away so soon after Robert's passing but she'd told them it was something she had to do; she'd promised their father she would. They'd accepted that. They'd not wanted to delve too deeply into her reasons for coming back to Vietnam. They'd heard Robert crying out from his nightmares through the years and she'd embarrassed them both during their awkward teenage phases more than once by shielding her head at a sudden noise or inexplicably crying at the smell of lemongrass in the supermarket.

Sally-Ann didn't want to tell them why she was going back either. It was always hard to imagine your parents having had a life before you came into it and sometimes your children were better off not knowing the ins and outs of that life.

She'd sensed their reticence at being back on the farm while they waited for the deed of sale to finalise. It was a place they'd both been eager to leave and see beyond. She understood. She'd felt the same once, too. The world was a big place and the boundaries of life on a rural sheep farm could feel as restricting as the electric and woven wire fencing used to keep those sheep in. So, with Robert's funeral done and dusted, she'd driven them to the airport and hugged them close, her kiss goodbye her blessing. They'd been quick to accept her assurances that she'd be fine and she'd watched them board the plane that would take them back to their big city lives on the other side of the country waving until she thought her arm would drop off. She'd stayed to see the plane take off and as it taxied down the runaway, the speed growing until it was airborne, she'd felt very alone.

She startled as the bus rumbled into life and the travel weary looking backpacker who'd obviously overslept stumbled down the aisle, her pierced midriff on display. She grasped hold of the seat in front of Sally-Ann's with an apologetic smile. She managed to smile back at the young woman as she steadied herself before continuing down the aisle. Hers was a freedom she and Robert had never known in their youth although they'd both sought adventure. How naïve she'd been back then.

She felt a pang for those lost years. The innocence of youth had been snatched from them by the reality of war and they'd both had to grow up brutally fast here. The dewiness of early adulthood had dried up in this place just like the lush green jungle of the countryside had withered and died. She'd seen the brown arid land burnt by Agent Orange spraying and fields filled with moon like craters from the B52 bombs dropped like rain from her vantage point in an old workhorse Hercules. Now her eyes flitted to the window opposite her. The glass was smeared with dust giving the world beyond a sepia tone. She stared but didn't see as they began to nose their way down the congested streets and as the smell of Arpège wafted up the aisle teasing her senses, she found herself back at the beginning.

Chapter 10

1967

'But why, Sal, I don't understand?' Terri's eyes, violet coloured mirrors of Sally-Ann's were wide. She stopped nibbling on the cheese sandwich letting it drop on the brown paper bag on her lap. Its crusts would curl in no time in the dry heat of this particularly hot summer's day, despite the shade from the gazebo under which they were sitting. Sally-Ann, on a rare weekend home from the Royal Perth Hospital where she was soon to complete her nurses training, had whisked her sister away from her Saturday morning job at Woolworths for lunch. She'd slapped together a hastily made picnic of Mum's tangy sheep's milk cheese sangers, apples, and a thick slab of homemade pound cake for afters. The scent of the roses wilting under the hot sun drifted by and Terri waved her hand in annoyance at the buzzing flies keen to investigate what was on the menu. 'Is it Billy?'

Sally-Ann made a choking sound and she too abandoned her sandwich even though she adored Mum's cheese. It was buttery soft and creamy, and one of the best things about coming home in her opinion. 'Billy Brown? No! He only had one thing on his mind and I wasn't interested. He's not the settling sort, Terri, and besides I'm not ready to settle.' Billy worked on the railway and she'd met him at a dance. He had a cheeky larrikin way about him that told her he'd be fun and he was, but he wasn't the sort of man you'd want to get serious about.

'Then why? You said you'd come home to Katanning to work in the hospital here when you finished your training.'

'And I will, just not yet.' Sally-Ann felt guilt poking its finger at her. Her sister was five years younger. It was a big gap when you were little but that gap had closed over the years and now at twenty-one Sally-Ann considered her sister her best friend. Mum had told the story often enough of how she'd refused to have anything to do with baby Terri when she'd brought the swaddled bundle home from the hospital. Her nose had been properly out of joint having had five years of Mum all to herself. Terri, however had adored her big sister from the get-go. Her enormous eyes, the exact same unusual shade of indigo as her own, a source of comment and compliments all their lives, would follow Sally-Ann's every move. As she got bigger, she'd howl of a morning when her sister banged the fly-screen door shut behind her, on her way to get the bus for school. She didn't know when it had changed. Mum reckoned it was when Terri began teething and the only person she'd be comforted by was Sally-Ann. She'd been her little sister's protector, confidante, and partner in crime ever since.

Should she tell her sister about Elsie the lovely old nurse who had taken a shine to her when she'd first arrived at the Royal Perth? Elsie had recognised her homesickness, and taking her under her wing, had assured her it would pass. Sally-Ann hadn't believed her at first; leaving home was an unexpected wrench she'd felt physically. She missed the wide, open expanse of flat land from her bedroom window and the sunsets she'd taken for granted each evening. She even missed Bessie's incessant barking of a morning as she waited for Dad to take her out on the rounds of the farm.

Elsie was right though and she'd soon made friends with the other nurses settling in to the new routines of life in the nurses' hostel. She'd even begun to enjoy the buzz of being in the big city. Of course she missed Terri, and Mum's cheese! She went home whenever she could manage it, knowing it was harder for her sister. Sally-Ann was busy having new and exciting experiences, she was learning and being challenged whereas for Terri life was exactly the same only her sister wasn't there to talk to at the end of each day.

It was Elsie who'd told her the world was bigger than Katanning. She'd nursed in Japan during the war and Korea too. She suggested given the intensive care experience Sally-Ann was gaining from her training she should put it to good use and join the army. Elsie said that she'd be married with children wrapped around her legs before she knew it and that she should go, see a bit of the world first. At first Sally-Ann had thought the idea was ridiculous. The army wasn't for the likes of her she'd told Elsie. She was a country girl whose home was where her heart was. Elsie had argued that she was strong, kind, and compassionate, exactly the sort of girl the army would be glad to have.

Elsie's words gnawed at her and each time she went home to Katanning, to the familiar rhythms of life on the sheep farm, she knew were she to leave nothing would change. It would be as it was when she returned. Nothing would change in the town either. The heritage rose gardens across the road from the town hall where she and Terri were sitting now, the

Pioneer Women's clock tower, the familiar shops and main street, they wouldn't change. It would all be here just the same when she got back, only she wouldn't be the same because she'd have done something different, seen new things. Her feet grew increasingly itchy until she found herself sitting here now trying to explain to her sister why she'd enlisted.

She was desperately trying to put all of this into words for Terri who was nodding like she understood but whose trembling bottom lip told a different story.

'It's not forever, Terri, I just need to spread my wings for a while. I'll be back before you know it.'

THE BUS SWERVED VIOLENTLY jolting Sally-Ann back to the present. The driver slammed his hand on the horn letting the man behind the wheel of the minivan veering too far over into their lane know what he thought of his road skills. If only she'd known what had lain ahead of her she thought, knowing that even if she had she still wouldn't have done things any differently.

Chapter 11

Present

Maureen did feel bad; no Mammy likes to see their daughter with a sticky pink eye. They'd go to a pharmacy and get some antibiotic drops as soon as they got to Nha Trang. Her own eyes were like sandpaper but that was from lack of sleep. She wasn't a natural early riser and neither was Moira. It was a good job they'd had reception give them a wake-up call or they'd both still be sound asleep. She glanced around her, catching the eye of a woman who looked like she'd spent a lot of time in the sun over the years. Her skin was a weathered, freckled brown which made her cornflower blue eyes all the more startling. Maureen liked cornflowers and she shrugged and smiled her 'Kids, who'd have em' smile at her'. The woman smiled back before turning away and Maureen settled herself into her seat before opening her day pack to retrieve her travel journal.

The bus was around three-quarters full now she noted, looking up to see a young woman clambering aboard mumbling her apologies and flashing her ticket. Her hair was terribly matted and could do with an introduction to a hairbrush. The bus juddered into life and the girl nearly went flying, reaching out and grabbing the seat in front of the woman with the cornflower eyes to steady herself. That was when Maureen noticed what she was wearing. She elbowed Moira.

'Ow, what was that for?'

'Look,' she fizzed excitedly.

Moira peered around her mammy to see a girl a year or two younger than herself. A bit of a hippy type she mused unsure what she was supposed to be looking at. She liked her nose piercing, not that she'd ever be game to pierce anything other than her ears. She had her belly button pierced too. Andrea had had that done. She said it wasn't the needle that hurt but the clamp used to hold the skin firm. It had made Moira feel sick just thinking about it. It was then her gaze drifted down and she saw what had Mammy all worked up. The woman was wearing identical elephant pants to the ones Aisling had shoved at her and fair play to her, they looked class. She could feel Mammy's eyes gleeful and triumphant on her.

'Do you think I'd look good with the dreadlocks then? It would save a fortune on shampoo and visits to the hair salon, so it would.'

'Don't be obtuse, sure they're an invitation for the mice to move in, so they are.'

Moira's lips formed a thin straight line. The insides of her thighs were still stinging and yer hippy one had managed to rock the pants. It wasn't as if she'd see anyone she knew while she was here, either. 'Alright then. What goes on tour stays on tour, yes?'

Maureen's nod was emphatic.

'Shake on it.'

'Shake.' She shook her daughter's hand. 'What am I shaking on?'

'I'll wear the fecking pants. When the bus pulls in for a comfort stop, I'll change into them but you are not—read my lips, Mammy—NOT to tell Aisling I wore them. I won't have her saying I told you so, understood?'

'Understood.' Maureen was already mentally penning her postcard to Aisling. In the meantime though, she'd update her travel journal. They'd gone to bed early last night what with the ungodly hour they'd had to get up this morning and she'd not had a chance to write in it. She wanted to fill it in while things were still fresh in her mind because one day when this trip seemed like it had all been a dream, she could pull it out and relive it all though her own words. She pulled the tray on the back of the seat down and set about writing.

Mammy's Travel Journal

WELL NOW HERE I AM sitting on the hop on, hop off bus. It's bit of a ramshackle old thing as though it should have been retired to wherever it is retired buses go a while back. It runs though and we're going to be hopping off at Nha Trang. We've another long day ahead of us as we're not due to arrive until dinnertime but sure we can put our feet up for a good few days once we get there. We had a grand day yesterday on a tour we booked at the same time as we bought our bus tickets. The minivan picked us up outside the Dong Do at eight o'clock and our driver, Duc, took a shine to Moira and insisted she sit up the front with him. I think he felt sorry for her because she's walking a bit bow-legged at the moment and what with the pink eye, she's a sorry sight. Serves her

*right, the bow-legged bit anyway, I say. At least she's seen sense
and agreed to wear the elephant pants.*

*It took a long time to get out of the city. Hoi Chi Minh, Duc
told us is home to over six million people. Imagine that, the whole
of Ireland has less than four million people living in it! The sprawl
just went on and on and once we were on the highway the potholes
in parts were spine jarring. I'm glad I brought a sturdy bra with
me but I will have to have a word with Moira. It might be hot but
she'll regret it when they're down around her middle in another
ten years. Perky is as perky does.*

*My first glimpse of the mighty Mekong River was a little
disappointing. Sure, it was a big sea of a river but it looked about
as clean as the Liffey only there were no shopping trolleys in this
one. An American woman, she had enormous teeth—I kept
thinking of the wolf in Little Red Riding, told me it's because of
the sediment from the surrounding countryside and the rocks that
sit along the bottom of it. It's the colour of stewed tea being poured
from a pot. We got on a long boat next. There were no life jackets
that I could see but I forgot all about that once we motored off.
Wooden stilt houses were dotted all along the banks and we passed
lots of boats with lone fishermen casting their nets. Moira took
loads of photographs. It was very peaceful although I did wonder
how they get on with toilets and the like because I couldn't see any
signs of plumbing under the houses.*

*We got off the boat at a market. I tell you nobody would ever
go hungry here not with all the fruit and vegetables for sale, there
was lots of shouting and bartering going on. All the women were
wearing the conical hats. I quite fancy buying myself one because
they'd keep the sun off your head a treat but at the same time,
they're as light as a feather which would save you from the hat*

hair at the end of the day. Moira said I'm on my own if I do. We shared some fresh pineapple and had a stroll around, well she swaggered more than strolled. I don't think I'll be eating much in the way of chicken not after seeing all those birds, freshly plucked, sitting out in the heat with the flies paying them a visit.

We got back on the boat and motored across to a place called Turtle Island where we trekked through the bush. I told Moira I was delighted my rambling training was already coming in handy. We came to a clearing where lunch was laid out and so we sat surrounded by mangroves and under a canopy of banana trees and had the tofu with noodles followed by fruit. I'm not really a tofu sort of a person but it was quite tasty. I kept saying 'Can you believe we're sitting under a banana tree, Moira,' because I really couldn't believe it. I don't think she could believe it either.

After lunch we got back on the boat and putted down a stream. It was very pretty with the sunshine dappling through the bamboo. We made a stop to visit a shop making banana wine and coconut sweets. I bought a packet of the fudgy sweets which was a mistake because I couldn't stop eating them. Very moreish they were but I felt sick once I'd finished the bag. A little further on we came to a village where we had honey tea and listened to traditional music.

Now, I'll be honest here, I thought Aisling's musical attempts as a child were appalling. I had to resort to bribery to try and get her in to the St Teresa's choir but not even my Porter Cake could sway those nuns. This, however, was something else it was like listening to a classroom full of children playing the recorder for the first time. Of course I smiled away and tapped my foot the way you do and even though it hurt my ears all the different musical instruments were very interesting. Oh and there was a snake in the café too. Two of the braver members of our group posed for photographs with it. It was green and yellow and kept hissing. Moira and I both said, NO thank you very much when it was waved our way.

It was a long, sleepy ride back to our hotel and over our early dinner of Vietnamese pancakes which didn't cause me any intolerance problems, although the chilli sauce was a bit hot for my liking. Moira and I agreed our day trip had been very good value. I thought we were rubbing along quite nicely, Moira and me, but then she woke up this morning with the pink eye and got very angry, accusing me of helping myself to her eye make-up. I've let her have the window seat on the bus and I think she's forgiven me. I'm not sure if it's a good idea writing this on the bus because it is very bumpy and I'm beginning to feel bilious.

'LOOK, MAMMY.'

Maureen must have nodded off because she started awake at the sound of Moira's voice. 'What is it? Are we there?'

'No, but look out there at the rice paddies it's so pretty and over there, see, I think it's some sort of cow.'

'It's a water buffalo, so it is.' Maureen sat up shaking off the drowsy fog of being on the road. The colours outside were glorious shades of green and gold and as they bounced through a village, the children, their faces bright with smiles came and stood in their doorways waving out to them.

'Ah bless.' Maureen wasn't sure that it was a good idea Moira peering out the window at the wee dotes the way she was, she'd frighten them with that eye but she decided it might be wise to hold her tongue on the matter. A particularly deep pothole saw her cross her legs. 'I hope we stop soon; I need to pay a visit. It's all this bouncing around.'

It was another twenty minutes before the bus rumbled into a lay-by. There was a restaurant with a toilet off to the side. Maureen did a silent head count of those ahead of them through narrowed eyes. 'Moira don't mess about getting off and when you do make a run for it.'

Chapter 12

The waves shushed up the beach in an almost hypnotic manner. Maureen and Moira were sitting at a table beneath gently swaying palm trees beside a breezy restaurant. On the other side of the restaurant was the promenade where, Moira had read in their guide book, American soldiers used to hold cyclo races. A postcard Maureen had just written to Noah was leaning up against the plastic napkin container and Moira had abandoned her good intentions of penning the promised cards to Andrea and her New Zealand friend, Tessa, in favour of watching the sunset.

The sky was awash now with hazy purples and pinks and the sun, a giant orange orb slipping slowly beneath the line where the silver sea and sky merged. The sticky heat of the day had dispersed and the light wind wafting in from the water gently caressed them. 'This is bliss so it is,' Maureen sighed happily waiting for her order of baked baby clams to arrive before taking a sip of her fruit juice. She'd have quite liked a Pina Colada but didn't think it would be fair to wave it under Moira's nose. 'I always feel like I'm on holiday when I see a palm tree.' *And sip on a Pina Colada*, she added to herself.

'Mmm,' murmured Moira soaking up the scene spread out before them. Her eye was already beginning to feel better thanks to the drops they'd picked up as soon as they'd gotten off the bus. Although she still had to resist the urge to rub at it. She stifled a yawn, it had been a long day and the roads in parts on the journey here had been bad, nerve-janglingly so, but they'd made it and she'd seen things along the way she'd never seen before. Sugar cane plantations, rice paddies, water buffalo, and houses with tin roofs that looked like they'd tumble down with one good gust of wind. What had struck her though was how all the people they'd seen as they'd rumbled alongside their farms or through their villages, had looked so content. Happy with their lot. People didn't look like that in cities she'd realised. They were always striving for more as they rushed off to somewhere important they had to be. It had felt, sitting on that bus today, as though time itself had slowed down.

She gazed out toward the beach. Ah, Jaysus but it was beautiful and she wondered briefly what Andrea was doing back home now. She'd tried but couldn't wrap her head around the time difference and had no idea if she'd be at work or fast asleep. Her mind drifted to Mason Price; had anybody done anything gossip worthy at the work's drinks she'd missed on Friday? To her surprise, she found she didn't really care. If people had nothing better to talk about than who was riding who, then they weren't really living were they? This was living she thought, and it dawned on her that for the first time in a very long while she felt as though she didn't have a care in the world. Well not quite, she did still have the pink eye and she'd have to make sure to hide her Elizabeth Arden exfoliating wash from Mammy for the rest of the trip. Oh and she would like to know if Andrea had given Jeremy from IT the glad eye after a wine or two. She'd done her best planting the seeds where he was concerned in an effort to sway her friend away from her unrequited love. She'd seen a few internet cafes around Hoi

Chi Minh there was bound to be one here somewhere to check her e-mail.

One thing was certain, whatever Andrea was up to right now she wouldn't be sitting by the seaside sipping coconut juice fresh from the shell in a singlet top with a pair of elephant pants on. She glanced down at them and ran her hand over the soft cotton fabric. They'd grown on her since she'd slipped them on in that nightmare of a toilet stop on the way here. She'd had to do a veritable Irish dance just to get the fecking things on without touching anything. The chaffing was a forgotten nightmare now and she liked how the pants made her feel ethnic, like she wanted to go get her belly button pierced and let her hair clump together in big knotty dreads. The idea of forgetting your real life and spending months tripping through Asia like that girl who'd been on their bus today was an appealing one. Of course, yer hippy woman didn't have Mammy by her side. She might not have looked so laid back if she had.

Moira had earwigged on the girl as she'd compared travel stories with the guy sitting across from her. The pair of them were kindred spirits, she'd thought, because his hair, having automatically checked him out as he'd boarded the bus also looked like it could do with a jolly good wash. She'd dismissed him with a big red cross when she caught sight of the wispy tufts of fluff protruding from his chin.

This poor attempt at a beard instantly reminded her of the old Ladybird book story Rosi used to read her, The Three Billy Goats Gruff, and she'd found herself doing the trip, trap, trip, trap bridge crossing bit in her head. Leather bracelets were wrapped around his wrist and somewhat disturbingly, she noted he had a pair of fisherman pants on just like Mammy's only his were orange. Mercifully Mammy was too busy rummaging in her pack to notice him otherwise she'd have felt obliged to let him know she too owned a pair only hers were green with gold swirly bits on them. She'd yet to break the pants out, too enamoured of her quick dry pants of many pockets.

Tom had mentioned when he asked her if she'd like to catch up when she got home, that he'd spent a lot of time backpacking around Asia. Had he worn pants like that fella's? Jaysus she hoped not, they wouldn't have done that lovely bum of his justice and he just wasn't the type to do the chin fluff thing. If he was, he wouldn't be her type at all. A scenario whereby she was in the throws of passion with him ensued, only for some reason he was wearing fisherman pants and she couldn't figure out how to get them off. It killed the moment and turning scarlet at the fact Mammy was sitting next to her and had always had an uncanny ability to read her mind, she'd diverted her thoughts by concentrating on the conversation going on behind her instead.

She'd heard them bandying words like full moon and the best beach ever about and envied them their carefreeness.

Now, a thought occurred to her. 'Mammy they have palm trees outside the Bloody Stream pub by the station in Howth. Is that why you like living there? Do you feel like you're on holiday whenever you wander around the harbour?' It would go a long way to explaining why her mammy had opted to move to the seaside village after Daddy died. There was something cathartic about palm trees; the sea and holidays, they were good for the health.

'No, I like being by the sea but sure those trees aren't proper palm trees like these.' She gestured to the spiky fronds above her head.

Moira spied a clump of coconuts and hoped that wind didn't get up. It wouldn't be a good look, being flown home on their travel insurance after being hit on the head by falling coconuts. 'Yes they are.'

'No, they're not, Moira. It's not a proper palm tree if you have to wear your Aran sweater and a vest to sit under it.'

They were diverted from pursuing this line of conversation by a lone woman, her face hidden by her conical hat, who was making her barefooted way up the beach toward them. Across her shoulders rested a stick, a basket dangling down either side. From where they were sitting and with the deepening dusk it was impossible to make out what she was on her way over to offer them.

'Say no, Mammy,' Moira muttered under her breath. 'N. O. It's not hard and sure, you've enough postcards to send Noah one once a week until his twenty-first and I do not want another coconut,' she gestured to the shell with the straw poking out of it, 'or a whole pineapple or papaya. Too much fruit gives me spots.' Spots she didn't need, not on top of the pink eye.

It was true, Maureen knew. She did find it hard to say no but the hawkers were very entrepreneurial in her book and it was so little to give and it obviously meant so much. She didn't have a tough streak like Moira. 'No' was a word she only used freely when it came to dealing with her children.

The woman reached them, her brown eyes twinkling and her smile broad as she relieved herself of her burden and gestured to the half full baskets. Moira didn't even look to see what was in them as she shook her head and said firmly, 'No, thank you.'

The arrival of Maureen's clams saved her from having to shake her head and the woman moved on. Moira eyed the open shells with distaste and wafted her hand back and forth across her face. 'They stink, Mammy.'

Maureen speared a crustacean with a fork and waggled it in her daughter's face. 'Do you want one?' Moira's face was shiny from the heat but she looked well she thought, eye aside of course. It was doing her good laying off the drink.

'No I do not.'

It had been a stroke of genius on her part insisting Moira join her on this trip, Maureen congratulated herself before popping the sweet, plump clam in her mouth.

Moira looked over at the restaurant pleased to see her omelette was on its way over.

'You'll turn into an egg the rate you're going,' Mammy said as the yellow omelette was placed in front of her along with a dish of chilli dipping sauce.

'I know where I'm at with an omelette even if it does have those beansprout things in it.' Some of the things she'd seen at the market in Hoi Chi Minh were unidentifiable and some like the rat kebabs were all too identifiable. No, an omelette was a safe bet and she tucked in, suddenly starving.

They cleaned up their plates in no time and decided to visit the night market. Maureen was mesmerised by the brilliant colours of the lacquerware boxes and vases on display, one stall stocking much the same as the next while Moira was like a moth to the flame with the lanterns. In her mind she was already turning her bedroom into a moody boudoir lit by deep purple and pink lanterns.

'Over my dead body,' Mammy stated as Moira put voice to her interior decoration aspirations.

As it happened neither woman was up for the haggling involved with making a purchase and Moira knew she was going to have to offload some of the gear she'd carted with her if she wanted to bring anything home. She'd only just sneaked in under the luggage allowance as it was. They were both beginning to yawn their heads off and in mutual agreement set off down the bustling streets to the hotel the bus had dropped them at.

Vietnam, Moira had noticed, came alive after dark. It must be down to the heat; hot countries were like that; look at Spain. They all napped in the middle of the day and didn't eat their dinner until ten o'clock at night. Music was pumping out onto the street as they passed by bars spilling over with young backpackers. She felt a strong urge to abandon her mammy and join them, especially as a fine young thing with shaggy blond hair grinned over at her. He reminded her of Tom. If she'd been here with Andrea, she knew she'd of been in the thick of all that, holding court. Her days would be spent lounging on the beach sipping cocktails, proper ones not kiddie style mocktails, and getting the odd massage. There'd be none of this chafing business, not because she was getting attached to the elephant pants but because she'd be relaxing not being herded about by that make-up thief Mammy of hers.

She trudged along as Mammy twittered on about whether the electric blue lacquered vase she'd been particularly drawn to would suit her sideboard or whether it might look a tad garish.

'Sure, that was the problem wasn't it? It was class alright but sometimes something that looked wonderful on holiday could look ridiculous once home.' Moira had bitten her tongue as she flashed back to the fisherman pants worn for high tea at Powerscourt. This wasn't right, she huffed to herself. She was twenty-five years old and willingly heading back to their hotel room for an early night—hanging around a person of sixty was making her act like one.

Chapter 13

Postcards

D*ear Noah,*
    The picture on the front is of the beach here in Nha Trang. You'd like it here because the beach is sandy and perfect for building sandcastles.

Moira paused, pen in mid-air. What would interest a five-year-old boy? Sure, he wouldn't want to know about gorgeous sunsets and cute, shaggy-haired backpackers. She thought for a moment longer and then it came to her. Little boys liked revolting things.

I have seen lots of things since we arrived in Vietnam. Rat kebabs for one thing! Can you imagine that? I've also had my photograph taken by a helicopter and your Nana had hers taken by a fighter plane. Tonight I drank from a straw straight from a coconut. It was delicious. Your nana ate seafood straight from the shell. It was gross. Tomorrow I'm going to go exploring and swimming. Be good for your mam.
    Love Aunty Moira

DEAR AISLING,
    It's your mammy here. Moira and I are in Nha Trang by the seaside. We're getting along surprisingly well and had a grand

time exploring Hoi Chi Minh once we got the hang of crossing the roads. It's very busy so it is, there's ten million registered motorbikes in Vietnam and the traffic is terrifying. It was nice to get away from the busyness of it all to visit the Mekong River. The tour we booked was very good value and I enjoyed seeing the stilt houses along the banks of the river. Poor Moira's struggling with the heat and she had a terrible bout of the chafing. Don't tell her I'm after telling you but she's wearing the elephant pants and thinks they're the best thing since sliced bread. She's always been the same, won't listen to advice and has to learn the hard way but sure, that's Moira. Tell Bronagh and Mrs Flaherty I've cards in the post to them too.

Love Mammy

MAUREEN PUT HER PEN down on the bedside table and flexed her fingers. They were cramping from all the news she had to write. She slid the postcards back into the brown paper bag before stuffing it in her pack, away from Moira's nosy gaze, ready for posting in the morning.

Their accommodation was nothing flash but it was neat and tidy and there was an en suite. She'd told Moira as they'd inspected the room that she'd stayed in a guesthouse in Italy once with a shared bathroom and it had been a nightmare. This room, she'd said, looking for dust balls under the bed and finding none, would do them nicely. Moira with that ridiculously oversized pack of hers had just been grateful to dump it on the bed.

Now, she heard the shower turn off and set about digging out her pyjamas, she was looking forward to a nice cool shower to freshen up before bed.

MOIRA CAREFULLY PUT the drops in her eye before exiting the bathroom. Her mood was somewhat improved now she'd washed the stickiness of the day away. There was nothing wrong with retiring early. Sure it wasn't a crime to be sensible just because she was young. She wasn't missing out on anything she hadn't done hundreds of time before and she was worn out after the ridiculous time she'd fallen out of bed this morning. An early night was just the ticket, she told herself pulling back her sheets. She clambered into bed to wait for Mammy to finish her ablutions and a short while later she appeared, smelling of toothpaste as she yawned widely. By mutual agreement they flicked off the lights.

Moira lay in the darkened room listening to the honks, shouts, and revving engines below. The walls were paper thin and she didn't know how she was supposed to drift off with all of that going on. When she was little a story had always helped send her off. What was the harm in asking? She rolled over on to her side propping herself up by an elbow. 'Mammy?'

'Mmm'

'Are you awake?'

Maureen smiled, as the memory of her youngest daughter standing silhouetted in the doorway of the bedroom she and Brian had shared at O'Mara's for most of their married life sprang to mind. Only back then when she'd appear, she'd be frightened having heard a creak or a groan she couldn't explain away. 'There's no monster under the bed, Moira. Old buildings make lots of night time noise, go on back to bed.' Maureen would murmur knowing it was pointless even as she pulled back the covers so her baby could clamber in beside her.

She could remember the feeling of that warm little body spooned into hers and how she'd tried to imprint the feeling of it on her memory. She knew too well how fast the time went. You blinked and your children were nearly grown, too big for middle of the night sleepy cuddles.

'Mammy,' she whined now. 'I can't sleep will you tell me a story.'

'Moira you're twenty-five.'

'I still want a story, c'mon tell me how you met Daddy.'

'Ah sure, you've heard that old chestnut a hundred times.'

'Ah, please, Mammy, it's been ages.' Moira liked the story. Hearing her mammy tell that particular tale was like that feeling you got sliding into bed in the middle of winter when the electric blanket had been warming it. '*Please*, I promise I won't mention you stealing my make-up ever again.'

'I didn't steal it. I borrowed it.'

'Pretty, please with a cherry on top.'

'Ah, go on then.'

Moira snuggled down under the bedding in anticipation.

Chapter 14

'Things were very different back then, Moira, you're talking the nineteen fifties.'

'The dark ages when you were lucky to get an orange in your stocking come Christmas and nobody knew what a computer was.'

'The cheek of it.'

'Sorry, carry on.' She liked hearing about where Mammy had grown up and her grandparents because they'd both passed on before she was born, not that they'd been a big part of their daughter's life once she'd left home. Moira had gleaned this from the bits and pieces she'd strung together over the years. Mammy didn't have much to do with her brothers either. This made Moira a little sad. She'd always thought it would be nice to be a part of her uncles' lives and to get to know all their cousins properly but it had never happened.

'Well as you know I grew up in the village of Ballyclegg in Connemara and my da was a farmer. He was a stern man, with the blackest of eyes and when he'd fix you with a certain look you'd quake in your boots. I don't recall him smiling very often, nor Mam for that matter. They were an arranged marriage, but I don't think that was the problem.'

'I can't believe that used to go on, arranged marriages and in our family too.'

'I'm sure there's loads worse gone on if you dig deep enough. Most families have all sorts of skeletons hiding in their cupboards. Sure look at my friend, Kate, she found out her mammy's youngest sister, whom she'd grown up thinking had passed on was locked away in one of those awful Magdalene laundries.'

It was true enough, what Mammy said, Moira supposed.

'I don't think it would have mattered who my mam and da married, they still wouldn't have smiled a lot. They just weren't smiley sorta people, so, I suppose in that way they were well suited. And you know, as a Mammy myself I can see the benefits of sorting out your children's spouses for them. I'd have saved you all a lot of messing so I would. I'd have found you a man with pots of money to keep you in the style you seem to think you should be accustomed to and I'd have had Aisling and Quinn together years ago. There'd of been none of that shilly-shallying around each other. Oh, and I'd be giving Pat's Miss Pneumatic Bosoms the heave-ho.'

Moira giggled. 'What about Rosi and Colin then?' She pulled a face in the dark at the thought of her chinless eejit of a brother-in-law. Their pairing was one Moira had never understood. There was Noah's arrival eight months after the wedding, but sure in this day and age getting pregnant didn't mean you were named and shamed if you didn't have a ring on your finger. Mammy was silent for a beat obviously not wanting to put her foot squarely in it which made a change, Moira mused.

'No, I don't think I would have picked him for our Rosi, but they muddle along well enough and if she hadn't of met Colin, then we wouldn't have Noah.'

There was that, Moira thought thinking of her nephew's chubby and highly kissable cheeks. 'But I don't want to muddle along.'

'Don't be all sanctimonious now. You were doing a grand job of it not long ago.'

'Ah, Mammy, just get on with the story.' Moira didn't want to think about Michael.

'Alright then. Now, where was I? Ah yes, well in our little cottage where the air was always smoky from the turf fire there was one rule growing up for my four brothers and another for me. I was expected to help Mam with the housework and the cooking while those lazy eejits didn't lift a finger about the place other than to eat or to fight.'

'Like Patrick then, Mammy?'

'No, not like Pat, he did his fair share.'

'Of not a lot.' Moira mumbled.

Maureen ignored her she was getting into the swing of her story now. 'Mam was a firm believer that a woman's place was in the kitchen. Whereas, I was not. It caused many an argument between us which usually resulted in me being made to wash my brother's dirty football togs in water from the rain barrel. I hated that. Can you believe that, Moira? No running water in the house. Things were so different back then. Children, especially girls, were seen as possessions of their parents and weren't expected to be independently minded. I don't think Mam knew what to do with me and all my opinions.'

'It sounds awful, Mammy.'

'No, not awful. It was just the way it was. I wouldn't say I had an unhappy childhood just not a particularly happy one. I don't remember an awful lot of laughter in our house. And you know all the children in Ballyclegg, apart from the family in the big house on the hill, we all came from not a lot. If I were to stick my head in the cottage next door and the one next to that to see what they were having for their tea it would be the same as ours. It was stew on a Monday, leftovers Tuesday, and bacon and cabbage on Wednesday—you could smell the cabbage as you wandered up the road from school and if you'd any doubts as to what day it was, you'd know it was Wednesday— and so it went. We all had the same so no one ever felt hard done by. I think it's probably why I spoiled you children.'

'We weren't spoiled.' Moira was indignant as she thought of every injustice ever served up by her parents growing up. Admittedly she could count them on one hand but still, spoiled? No way. Sure, hadn't she begged her mammy for the boots from Korky's to no avail when she was fifteen years old, an age when the kinda boots you wore really mattered.

'You'll see what I mean, when you have babies of your own, Moira. I mean didn't we take you on a grand family holiday around the Ring of Kerry when you were small? And we had some lovely weekends in Rosslare. In my day we had to walk everywhere and the only place Mam and Da ever took us was church on a Sunday.'

Moira remembered the trip around the Ring of Kerry. She'd been violently carsick all over poor Rosi. Patrick was about to move out and goodness knows what her parents had bribed him with to make him join them, but come along for the ride he had. Her sisters too were at an age where it was friends first, family second, and so Mammy and Daddy did the unheard of and took time off from running O'Mara's in order for them to have one last hurrah all together as a family.

'The only time I left Ballyclegg growing up was on a school trip to Dublin and I had to beg and beg to be allowed to go. I was so excited about it I threw up half an hour before I had to leave for school to get the bus and Mammy very nearly didn't let me go. I always felt bilious when I got too excited as a child. It was a terrible thing because sometimes I'd miss out on whatever had me in such a state altogether on account of being sick. Anyway, I knew the moment we arrived in the city and I saw the busy streets all bursting with life that I'd live there one day.'

'And you did.'

'And I did, but it wasn't an easy path I chose to take. My future was mapped out for me like Mam's had been. I mean they hadn't gone so far as to find me a match but I knew they had their eye on the Doyle family's son, Gerry. I can tell you, Moira, I certainly didn't. He was a right eejit of a fella, as thick as a plank, and Jesus, Mary, and Joseph you'd want to have seen the teeth on him.' Maureen was silent for a moment lost in her memories. 'You know, I knew deep down that if I didn't leave the minute my schooling was done then I'd never leave and my life would play out exactly like Mam's only under a different roof. So one day, Moira, I did something very bad.'

Moira knew what she'd done but she still had to ask, it was all part of the story telling. 'What did you do, Mammy?'

'I stole the fare to Dublin and enough for a couple of nights lodging from Mam's tin and I got on that bone-rattling auld bus to the big smoke and I never looked back. Sure, when I thought about all those years toiling after my brothers with not so much as a word of thanks from them, it was only what I was owed anyway.'

Moira knew her mammy had sent the money back as soon as she'd earned it but what she'd done had soured family relations and things had been very strained between them all as a result. She couldn't imagine what it would be like to be estranged from your family. To not speak to Aisling every day when she was home or not to roll her eyes at something her mammy said at least twice a week. She took it for granted that she could pick up the phone and chat to Rosi and Noah whenever she wanted. Sure, Patrick was hit and miss these days but still she liked to think if she'd actually come right out and said to him she needed him, he'd have come. 'You were very brave.'

'I was, wasn't I? Although, Moira, when I look back now, I can't quite believe that I was that bold young girl. Risk taking is for the young.'

Moira didn't need the light on to know her mammy was shaking her head at the memories. 'It all worked out though, Mammy, and if you hadn't of left Ballyclegg you'd never have met Daddy and had us.'

'True enough I might have married Gerry Doyle and had a tribe of children all with teeth you could eat an apple through a tennis racket with.'

They both giggled at the image that conjured.

'What was it like arriving in Dublin? It must have been frightening not knowing anyone or having anywhere to go.'

'It was but I'd made my decision and I was determined I'd make a success of it. Although lying awake most of that first night in the awful lodging house I'd found, I wondered if I'd made a mistake. It was the first time I'd slept in a bed that wasn't my own and I didn't like the smell of the sheets. They were coarse too and made my skin itch. The noises of the city outside were so different to the noises of the country and I was full of the fear.'

Moira tried to visualise it but she always found it hard to equate her sensible, bossy Mammy with the free-spirited young woman who'd run away to Dublin, that she was describing.

'Everything looks brighter in the light of day though and come morning I resolved to find myself job. I set off with quite a spring in my step but by lunchtime my feet hurt and I found myself sitting in the middle of St Stephen's Green wondering what I was going to do. I hadn't counted on needing telephone experience or typing skills and I didn't even know what bookkeeping was.'

Moira held her breath. This was her favourite bit in the story. When Mammy first met Daddy. She was fairly sure she embellished bits and pieces but didn't care a jot.

'I sat there in the park watching the ducks swim lazily around for an age before I told myself that it was no good sitting on a bench feeling sorry for myself. All I'd accomplish was a bout of the piles, sitting in the cold like that. Watching the ducks wasn't going to find me work. So, even though there was a hole in the sole of my shoe and a blister on my heel, I got up and I made myself walk out the gates. Something, and it must have been fate, made me cross the road. It was as I was walking up the street admiring the tall, elegant manor houses I spied a sign in the window of a guesthouse.'

Moira found herself mouthing the words, 'Live-in housekeeper position available, only hard worker's need apply.'

'It was the answer to my prayers. I'd been housekeeping from the moment I could hold a broom in my hands. So, I opened the gate and marched up to the front door. I didn't see the peeling blue paint as I lifted the lion's head which was in need of some Brasso and elbow grease, and I rapped on that door. A young man opened it, he was very smartly turned out, and I stood there for a moment staring like the culchie I was because he was also the most handsome fellow I'd ever seen.

'You weren't exactly spoiled for choice in Ballyclegg by the sounds of it though, Mammy.'

'Shush, Moira, you're ruining the moment.'

'Sorry.'

'Right then, where was I?'

'He was the most handsome fellow you'd ever seen.'

'He was, and a fine set of teeth he had on him too. My stomach began to behave very strangely when he smiled at me and when he asked "Can I help you?" I hardly heard him. He had to repeat himself before I managed to say, "I'm here about the job in the window." Then I remembered to put on my brightest smile and my best foot forward. It was all well and good behaving like a love-struck fool but I needed a job. "Ah right," he said opening the door wider. "You'd better come in and meet my mam."'

'And then he went and fetched Granny O'Mara and you became her right-hand woman running O'Mara's and you and Daddy fell in love, got married and lived happily ever after in the Guesthouse on the Green,' Moira finished off the story feeling very satisfied with it all. She thought she might just be able to fall asleep now.

'Eventually, yes.'

No that was not how it went. Her eyes popped open. 'What do you mean, eventually?'

'Well, I went to Liverpool first.'

'What?' Moira pulled herself upright. This was news to her. So far as she knew Mammy had never left Ireland without Daddy and she'd had no idea she'd spent time in Liverpool. 'You never said.'

'I didn't see the need. You always liked the story to end when I met Daddy and moved in to O'Mara's. It was your fairy-tale ending.'

'But I thought that *was* where it ended.'

'Oh no, Moira, I hadn't left home to settle down. Sure, I was only seventeen. I wanted an adventure first.'

Chapter 15

1954

Maureen Nolan closed the door on the lodging house behind her and set off down Parliament Street. The purposeful confidence to her step belied the uncertainty she was feeling. She'd only been in Liverpool three days and the busy streets were new and unfamiliar and more than a little exciting! She kept her brisk pace up, passing by the imposing Liverpool Cathedral before heading down Upper Duke Street, as per her landlady's instructions, not daring to dawdle and risk being late for her interview.

She'd landed on her feet with her lodgings, and was grateful to Mr Drinkwater, a travelling salesman with a roving eye who'd spent a few nights at O'Mara's, for his recommendation. A few years older than her he'd seemed rather worldly to her inexperienced eye as he leaned against the wall in reception while she manned the front desk. He'd been in no hurry to head up the stairs to his room as he stood gloating about the talent competition, he'd taken part in at the Grafton Ballroom in the heart of Liverpool. The hall was apparently a popular nightspot in the Merseyside city, a regular port of call of his, and one he made certain to visit each time he parked his shoes in Liverpool. The girls, he'd told her, smoothing his quiff, had flocked around him upon hearing his version of Sinatra's *New York, New York*. Ol' Blue eyes had nothing on him he'd winked before offering to demonstrate his singing prowess but Maureen had told him, there was no need, she'd take his word for it.

He might have been an arrogant so and so but his banter got those feet of hers itching again. The wanderlust had lain dormant while she'd being working at O'Mara's. Her days had been full as she beavered alongside Mrs O'Mara learning the ropes of running a guesthouse. She'd not sat around twiddling her thumbs on her days off either. Brian was always on hand, seemingly happy to take her out and about even if it was at his mammy's suggestion. She was half in love with him, she knew that. She had been from the first moment he'd ushered her inside his enormous family home the day she'd come knocking about work but if the feeling was reciprocated then he'd yet to play his hand.

She would spend those afternoons when they were together imagining what it would be like to have his brown eyes with their flecks of gold gaze into hers before his soft lips descended on hers. He hadn't given her any sorta sign that he saw her as anything more than, well, than a kid sister, apart from the time he'd held her hand. She hadn't known whether it was because he thought she needed help crossing busy Dame Street or whether he'd wanted to feel her hand in his and he'd dropped it when they got to the other side.

That was the problem with Brian, nothing was clear, nothing at all, and perhaps she was wasting her time. Maybe he was just being kind by showing her the delights of old Dublin town. A girl couldn't wait around forever. She'd resolved to ask Mr Drinkwater where she could stay were she to want to spend time in Liverpool and perhaps visit the Grafton Ballroom herself.

Mrs Murphy's house he'd said, while in a colourful area, was safe enough so long as she kept herself to herself. It was a clean, central, and reasonably priced establishment and she could do a lot worse than staying at the home of the affable widow who cooked a damned good fry-up. Brian had come in from work then, smart in his suit and tie, and there was something about his bristling manner that had seen Mr Drinkwater peel himself off the wall and make himself scarce.

For Maureen though the seed had been planted. She'd left Ballyclegg determined not to moulder away her youth there and now she was feeling equally determined not to waste it by not going and seeing a bit of the world because she was too busy waiting for Brian O'Mara to decide whether he was half in love with her too. She'd handed her notice in, much to Mrs O'Mara's consternation, and tried not to be upset by Brian's silence where his feelings for her one way or another were concerned. He'd had his chance she resolved, clasping the worn old leather case that contained her worldly belongings to her chest as she tried to keep her lunch down while the ferry rocked and rolled its way across the Irish Sea.

Moira had liked Mrs Murphy immediately. She had a warmth about her that invited you in and made you want to stay. She'd told Maureen, she had a soft spot for the Irish given the late Mr Murphy could trace his roots back to County Clare. The older woman had taken her under her ample wings, recognising how green around the gills she was. She called her young Mo and this morning had filled her up on toast and porridge insisting she needed fattening up because if she

wasn't careful a gust of wind off the Mersey would pick her
up and blow her back to Dublin. It was Mrs Murphy who'd
directed her to the Labour Exchange the day before which had
resulted in her being handed a card to give to the Personnel
Manager this morning at Lewis's Department Store where she
was headed now. 'You'll know you're at Lewis's,' Mrs Murphy
said clearing her plate, 'when you see Dickie Lewis.' She'd
laughed at Maureen's expression and with a wink said, 'You'll
see what I mean.'

She recited the directions in her head, right onto Berry
Street, then follow it down to the end before veering left on to
Renshaw Street, this would take her to Ranelagh Street where
the store was. Maureen had worn her best white blouse and
new burgundy skirt with the tiny daisy pattern, she'd bought
just before leaving Dublin. She'd parted with her carefully
saved pennies in a last desperate bid to catch Brian's eye. It
hadn't worked, though she was certainly catching a few eyes
this morning, she thought, as a fella tipped his hat at her. She'd
cinched her waist in with a black waspie belt and had a
matching handbag. It pleased her to see she looked as
fashionable as any of the young women she'd seen thus far. She
held her head high nearly tripping over a loose paver in the
process!

There'd been so many different sights to see since arriving
a few short days ago. On her first morning venturing out she'd
bumped in to the first black person she'd ever seen. The spiced
smells drifting from open doorways had left her curious as to
what was for dinner and the sounds emanating from the houses
as she'd apologised to the man and gone on her way had danced

to a different beat too. It was one she'd never heard before and she liked it.

'Ah now, that would be calypso or perhaps jazz you heard, young Mo,' Mrs Murphy had said tossing the tea towel down on the bench before taking her hand and doing a little jive right there in the kitchen. 'I'm partial to a capella myself.' She'd had to explain what that was to Maureen.

The streets were alive this morning too, with men in suits and shoes you could see your face in, all checking their watches, briefcase in their other hand, as they strode to their offices. Young women in the latest fashions minced along and matronly head-scarfed early morning shoppers keen to secure a bargain joined in with the throng. A newspaper boy was doling out copies of the Liverpool Echo and a double-decker bus was disgorging its passengers on time for them to get to work and clock in. The air was a curious mix of diesel fumes, cigarette smoke and, if you inhaled sharply enough, you could detect a tang of salt from the nearby Mersey. Maureen felt dwarfed by the smog blackened buildings, seagull droppings adorning their ramparts either side of her. She shivered at the biting wind somehow sneaking its way in through the nooks and crannies of those buildings and was grateful for the white cardigan she'd thrown on at the last moment.

Her mind strayed to Brian, and she wondered what he was doing now. She tried not to think about him, she tried really very hard not to, but he'd creep into her thoughts unbidden more often than she liked. It was just after eight thirty so she supposed he'd be sitting at his desk now. He'd shown her the rather bland building where he worked as a draughtsman, a job he said he'd been steered into by his father who didn't want him reliant on the whim of holidaymakers. Had she been in Dublin she'd have been helping Mrs O'Mara with the breakfasts before setting about making up the vacated rooms. She'd liked the people side of the guesthouse business the best, had loved listening to their stories about the places they called home.

She supposed she could have sought hotel work or a housekeeping position here in Liverpool but she wanted to try her hand at something different. It was all part of her grand adventure. So, she was pleased when the po-faced man at the Labour Exchange had said that since she was obviously adept at dealing with the public, he'd put her forward for a position that had just become available at Lewis's.

She realised she was nearing Ranelagh Street and as she saw the imposing nine-storey building looming ahead of her, her mouth stretched in to a wide grin. She'd just spotted Dickie Lewis and she sent a silent thank you to Mrs Murphy because she was too busy giggling to herself to pay attention to the nervous flutterings of anticipation. There above the entrance to the department store was the statue of a man, his naked body there for all to see, arms flung wide as he stretched forward from the prow of a ship.

MAUREEN HAD BEEN EMPLOYED in the haberdashery department at Lewis's for exactly two weeks and was, thanks to her predecessor, now an authority on all things handbags, scarves, and stockings. She arrived to work each morning pinching herself at the elegance of her place of work enjoying the way her heels tip-tapped across the Italian marble tiled entrance floor.

As promised, she'd written to Mrs O'Mara full of news about her lodgings with Mrs Murphy and her new job. She'd filled a page telling her how, come Easter, her new friend Mary who worked in the food hall at the rear of the ground floor had told her the toy department would be transformed into a springtime wonderland. A farmyard was to be created for the children to come and admire with bales of hay and daffodils. There were to be chicks and miniature ponies and everything. Sure, the whole thing sounded just magical, she'd written. As for the Christmas grotto she'd heard tell of, well that was a whole other letter.

This particular morning, Maureen looked up from her discussion over the merits of different deniers to see a man standing at the top of the steps leading down to her floor. He had a hand thrust in his wide-legged trousers pocket as he stood with a casual nonchalance surveying the departments below for a few ticks. Then, cutting a dashing swathe past a woman with an impressive bouffant, he made his way toward the perfume counter where prim Miss Mottram was busying herself with a counter arrangement.

He looked like Rock Hudson, Maureen decided, assuring the woman in her coat and headscarf that the nylons she was hemming and hawing over wouldn't ladder easily.

'They'd better not for the price, luv,' she said but Maureen barely heard her as she placed them in a bag and handed the woman her chit. She was too busy watching Miss Mottram fall all over herself. She positioned herself by the handbags so she could better observe their interaction.

Miss Mottram had sprayed a sample of something on to a card and was wafting it under his nose. He shook his head and she cocked her head to one side listening before retrieving another for him to sample. This one he seemed to like because she looked very pleased with herself as she retrieved a bag in which to place his purchase. Maureen sighed so wistfully a woman with a small boy clutching her hand asked her if she had the weight of the world on her shoulders. Maureen had laughed the comment off, but oh how she'd have loved a bottle of the French perfume and especially if it was given to her by a man with movie star good looks! She thought of Brian and pushed him away. It wasn't the sort of thing he'd ever do; he'd never even told her she looked well when she'd worn her new skirt. He just wasn't a French perfume sorta man.

At clocking off time, she and Mary, twins in their matching black and white uniforms, picked up their bags and linking arms left the building to join all the other workers making their way home at the end of a busy day. They crossed over Ranelagh Street and Mary cheekily blew a kiss at the Adelphi's doorman but his dour expression didn't change nor did he tip his top hat at her. She was a live wire, Maureen thought fondly before launching into her tale about the dreamy fella who'd bought a bottle of French perfume for his girlfriend. Mary agreed whoever she was, was one lucky lady and she laughed at Maureen's description of Miss Mottram giggling and carrying on like a schoolgirl and not a forty-something spinster.

'My feet are killing me, it's like little needles stabbing at them,' Maureen moaned. 'I thought I'd be used to being on my feet all day by now but they're aching, so they are. I don't know how I'll manage tonight, Mary.' They were meeting later at the

Locarno Dance Hall where a skiffle band contest was being held that evening. A fella Mary was sweet on who was handy with the washboard was going to be taking a turn on the stage with his band.

'Soak them in vinegar and warm water. It works a treat, Mo, and you'll be good as new by eight o'clock, I promise.' The two girls veered down the lane that would take them to the little Chinese restaurant they'd discovered did a tasty Thursday special of chicken and rice. It would do nicely for their dinner. Maureen wondered fleetingly what her parents would make of her frequenting a Chinese restaurant and the thought of the look on their faces made her smile. The smile vanished though as she recalled the curt letter she'd received in reply from her mam after she'd written to her enclosing the money she'd borrowed. She'd wanted to let her know she was safe and well and enjoying herself in Dublin, but her mam had told her she was a selfish mare who needn't bother showing her face in Ballyclegg again. It was what she'd expected but it still stung.

MAUREEN TAPPED HER red kitten-heeled shoes along to the beat, the vinegar had indeed rejuvenated her poor tired feet and she was itching to take a turn on the dancefloor. The six-piece band on stage might be amateurs, but they had rhythm and they were playing her favourite, Buddy Holly's *That'll be the Day*. The lad on the banjo was fantastic. The Quarrymen as they were called would go far, she thought fanning herself with her hand.

It was hot and crowded inside the dance hall. Maureen had lost sight of Mary half an hour ago when she went in search of her washboard player leaving her to stand on the side-lines soaking up the electric atmosphere. This was her first visit to the Locarno and she'd been in awe of its Tardis-like interior as Mary, giggling with excitement, had pulled her inside. She'd gushed that the elephants and other animal carvings adorning the walls were due to the ballroom having started life as a circus venue. She'd even said that hidden underneath the wooden dance floor was an elephant pit that had been home to the lions and elephants starring in the circus. Maureen's gaze fell to all those stamping feet on the dance floor and a feeling of trepidation stole over her lest the floor cave in. Ah, sure you're being silly Maureen Nolan, she told herself turning her imagination away from collapsing dance floors to Brian O'Mara. What would he make of it here? Did he like to dance? She didn't know.

'The perfume was for me ma in case you're wondering.' A broad scouse accent sounded in her ear sending a shiver ricocheting down her spine and she swung around startled. It was him, Rock Hudson, only instead of an American accent he had an unexpected Liverpudlian intonation. It was at odds with the picture she'd had of him in her head but she forgot all about that as he gave her a wink, 'I saw you today over by the handbags in Lewis's, luv.'

She could smell the minty gum on his breath as he chewed and eyed Maureen cheekily. She was glad of the dim lighting as she felt her face heat up at having been caught out.

'Are you dancin'?' he asked running his fingers through an Elvis like quiff.

Maureen kicked the door shut on Brian O'Mara as she replied, 'Are you askin'?' Just like Mary had told her she should before letting him take her by the hand to lead her into the melee.

Chapter 16

Present

'Mammy, stop right there. If this new version of the story finishes with you telling me that Patrick was in fact the secret love child of you and this Rock Hudson fella with the Elvis hair, I don't think I need to know.' Moira was feeling a little short of breath now sitting up in bed, her back pressed up against the wall. She couldn't believe the twists and turns of this story she'd thought she'd known from start to finish. 'What I want to know is where does Daddy fit? Because I'm beginning to wonder from the way you've been describing him if myself, and my sisters were conceived by immaculate, conception.'

Maureen laughed. 'I was a good girl I'll have you know, Moira. I kept my legs firmly crossed until my wedding night. You're always in such a hurry to get to the end of things. And the end is the best bit, you should savour it not hurtle along towards it.'

'Mammy, get on with it!'

'God Almighty, Moira, I'm getting there.' She cleared her throat. 'Yer man Rock, whose name was in fact, Len.'

Moira snorted, 'Len?'

'Yes, Len. Short for Leonard. What's wrong with that?'

'Nothing, Mammy, nothing at all.'

'Good, then stop interrupting. *Len* and I became an item. I was his bird as they say over the water and I was smitten. I forgot all about your father. Len worked for the newspaper as a machine manager and he knew all the fun places to dance away the weekend. Then, one day, ooh it would have been three maybe four weeks after we started courting, I arrived home from work. Mrs Murphy greeted me at the door with a peculiar look on her face and said, 'There's someone come to see you.' Well, standing there in the doorway I went hot and cold at the thought of it being my da come to fetch me back but when I went through to the kitchen, I couldn't believe my eyes because there, larger than life, was Brian. He was sitting at the table sipping a cup of tea with one of Mrs Murphy's teacakes in front of him.'

This was more like it thought, Moira. 'He'd come to whisk you back to Dublin.'

'He had, although he told me it was his mammy who sent him because she hadn't found anyone half as good as me to help out around the old place and would I please come back.'

'So you packed your bags and sailed off into the sunset with Daddy.'

'I did not.'

Moira, humphed in frustration.

'I told Brian, I had a good thing going on here in Liverpool and that I would be staying where I was thank you very much. I told him I was courting and he couldn't just bowl on up and expect me to leave my job, my fella, and my new home on the word of his mammy. No, I sent him off that evening with a flea in his ear although I did tell him to tell Mrs O'Mara I was sorry

I wasn't coming back. It wasn't her I was angry with after all. She was a lovely lady, your nan.'

Moira's Nana had passed away before she was born. She'd always felt cheated listening to the others reminisce about her. 'He can't have given up on you though, not unless we're all Len's love children and Daddy adopted us.'

'Would you stop harping on about love children? I told you I was a chaste girl; I didn't get up to any shenanigans until I was a married lady unlike you lot today. We weren't all free n easy in the fifties dropping our drawers willy-nilly. We had morals, so we did.'

'Nothing wrong with trying before buying, Mammy.'

'I'll pretend I didn't hear that, Moira O'Mara. Now then, do you want to know what happened next, or not?'

'Of course I do.' It was like reading a serial in a magazine, Moira thought with all the painful long breaks in between instalments.

'It was Mrs Murphy who brought Brian and me together in the end. She wasn't overly taken with Len. She didn't think he was right for me, too much of a wide-boy in her book. A flash Harry was the term she used I believe. She liked Brian though from the moment he complimented her on her teacakes. She reckoned she could see the pair of us were smitten with each other but apart from banging our heads together she wasn't sure what to do about it, and then it came to her. She recalled me telling her about the first time I saw Len. She stopped Brian at the door that evening as he made to leave with his tail between his legs. I'd flounced off to my room by then and before he went on his way, she told him how she thought I was the sorta girl who might be swayed in her thinking by a bottle of French perfume and how if he were to make a grand gesture along those lines he might persuade me to go back to Dublin with him.'

Moira felt a shiver of anticipation.

'When I arrived home from work the next night Brian was sitting at the kitchen table. At first, I thought he'd come back for more of Mrs Murphy's teacakes because I'd made it perfectly clear as to where I stood the day before. That wasn't why he'd come, although if I recall rightly, he did have a teacake in front of him when I—'

'Mammy!'

'Alright, alright. This time around, he'd come bearing a gift. He presented me with a beautifully wrapped box and what do you think was inside it, Moira?'

'A ring?'

'Jesus wept are you not listening to what I'm telling you. We hadn't even had our first kiss. No, it was a bottle of French perfume, you eejit. Arpège. Brian took hold of my hand and said, 'The woman on the counter told me it was a bold and beautiful floral fragrance and that made me think it was perfect for you.' And I melted right there on the spot. So, there you go Moira, that's when I packed my bags and sailed back to Dublin with him. You know the rest.'

'Are you crying, Mammy?'

'Happy memories, Moira, happy memories.'

'What about Len? He must have been heartbroken when you left.'

'I don't think so. Len moved on pretty smartly. I kept in touch with Mrs Murphy until she passed and she told me she'd heard down the line that he married a girl called Shirley. She said he'd got her in the family way which meant she'd been right about him all along, a wide boy, and hadn't I made the right decision by breaking up with him. The End. Now then, do you think perhaps we could try and get a spot of shut eye?'

Chapter 17

The sunlight sneaked in through the cracks in the curtains and on the street below Moira and Maureen's window, a street that had only gone to sleep a few hours ago, some arse was revving his bike. *Did these people never rest?* Moira thought opening her good eye. Jaysus, she muttered to herself, you'd think whoever it was, was about to take off in the Isle of Man TT with that carry-on.

Moira knew about motorcycle races, not because she had a love of speed but because at sixteen, she'd had a boyfriend who did. Callum or was it Ciaron? She couldn't remember now but either way he'd been obsessed with motorbikes and everything to do with them. It was at the end of their three months together that he'd shown up outside the guesthouse one Saturday morning on the only bike his motor mechanic's apprenticeship wage could afford—a gutless Yamaha. The relationship's death knoll had sounded because Moira had refused to be seen on the back of what she told him had less grunt than her hairdryer. He wasn't a keeper, she'd decided, as he'd revved his engine in her direction one final time before taking off in a blaze of backfiring exhaust fumes.

'Feck off, would ya,' she said now in response to the revving below. Mammy had begun to make those annoying little lip-smacking noises that signalled she was on the verge of waking up. Moira wondered how she'd be feeling when she did rise and shine; not too bright she guessed. She lay there a few beats longer, a seething mass of irritability as she debated whether she could summon the energy to get up and hang out the window to repeat the sentiment. She was not in fine fettle this morning. It had been a terrible night.

It had taken her forever to nod off, what with the ruckus coming from outside, but even if it had been silent, she knew she'd have had trouble getting to sleep. Mammy's story had unsettled her. She'd been unable to shake the 'what if's' of which there were many. They'd trotted themselves out one after the other as she'd lain there stewing.

What if Mammy had stayed in Ballyclegg and married yer bucktooth man? Or, what if she'd walked out Fusilier's Arch when she left St Stephen's Green that day and headed down Grafton Street instead of leaving through the south gates? She'd never have seen the sign in the window of O'Mara's and she'd never have met Daddy. She'd felt very peculiar at that point because it had occurred to her that if Mammy had been drawn toward the busy shopping street, instead of wandering past the row of Georgian buildings, she and her siblings wouldn't exist. It also occurred to her that she was reliving the film she'd seen last year with Andrea, the one with yer Paltrow woman in it. *Sliding Doors*. Very good it had been too.

Most of all though, she'd been disturbed at the twist the familiar old story of how her parents met had taken. It was a bit like listening to *Beauty and The Beast* only Beauty takes off from the big mansion where she's staying with yer Beast, goes and has a bit of a thing with the village blacksmith before coming back and marrying the Beast. Not that Daddy was a beast he was the handsome prince at the end of the story.

The very thought of her mammy being torn, she refused to say between two lovers because, well the 'l' word was not a word used when thinking about Mammy, typically indecisive was a better fit, well, it had shocked her. She knew what she was struggling with. It was trying to equate, Mammy, her mammy who'd always been part and parcel of the furniture at O'Mara's, ready to kiss a grazed knee better or hold out a hanky with which to blow a runny nose, with the young woman she'd been before she turned into Mammy. A young woman who'd been unafraid as she boldly went adventuring into new cities. A young woman who had men fancying the pants off her. I mean, it was *Mammy* for fecks sake! Yes it was all very unsettling, there was no other word for it she'd thought rolling over and thumping the rock of a pillow for the tenth time. That was when the groaning had started from the bed next to her.

'Mammy, what is it? Are you alright?' she'd hissed into the darkened room. She was annoyed with her for changing the story on her, she realised, finding it hard to muster up sympathy for whatever it was had her moaning. Sure, it was probably just indigestion or wind. She could be very dramatic at times.

'Oooh, Moira, my tummy's after doing some very unnatural things.'

She heard an unearthly rumble and grimaced. 'Jaysus, was that your stomach?'

'I can't talk. I've got to go.' Her tone was desperate and Moira heard her stampede to the bathroom, the light flickering on and illuminating her white face briefly before she kicked the door shut.

Moans, groans, interspersed with mutterings about fecking clams and never again, drifted out from under the door. You'd have to be inhuman listening to that and not feel sympathy, Moira thought clenching her cheeks in solidarity at the other sounds that surely the whole hotel would be privy to. She hoped nobody thought it was down to her when she ventured forth, that would be mortifying. It seemed to take an age but finally there was a flushing sound and she could hear the tap running as she washed her hands before the handle turned and Mammy reappeared.

'Ah, Moira, I'm just after losing half my bodyweight.'

'I'd believe it. Go back to bed and try to get some sleep. I'll get you something to settle your tummy from the pharmacy when they're open.'

'You're a good girl.'

The room had the hazy half-light that signalled daylight was on its way and Moira had watched as her Mammy buried herself under her bedding, before shutting her own eyes and finally drifting off.

That must have been around five o'clock, she thought now. Then, with one final humph in the direction of the window she kicked the sheets off and sat up. There was no point lying here, she'd be better off having a shower and then going in search of a cup of coffee. She made her way with trepidation to the bathroom which she'd already nicknamed the clam-room hoping Mammy had had the foresight to open the window. She eyed the hump under the bedclothes that was just beginning to stir, before pushing open the door. Her gaze flicked around the space checking it out like the gards with a warrant but all was as it should be apart from the trio of geckos who'd taken up residence on the ceiling thanks to the open window. She could feel their beady reptilian eyes on her while she showered. It was most unnerving.

The water revived her and she was pleased to see on inspection that her eye was much better today. She put the drops in and waited for her vision to clear before checking on Mammy. Maureen's tousled head was just visible above the sheets she'd wrapped around herself.

Moira laid her hand on her forehead which was reassuringly cool. She'd live. 'I'm going to go and find some breakfast, and I'll pick you up something to settle your stomach while I'm out. You'll be alright here for a bit.' There was a mumbling she took to be a thanks and, pausing only to open the window a crack to let some fresh air into the room, Moira headed out.

She felt quite adventurous. It was the first time she'd been on her own since they'd left Dublin and she should make the most of it. Be bold, like her mammy had been and explore. There was plenty of time for that though, first things first, coffee, food, an internet cafe and a visit to the pharmacy in that order.

The sun cleared away the last vestiges of her broken night and feeling invigorated she strode up the street toward the road where she knew she'd find everything she needed. Her nose wrinkled as she tried to ignore the pungent sewage smell that wafted up, seemingly from nowhere, stagnating in the humid air. She was determined it wouldn't put her off her breakfast. Across the street she saw a woman, her face hidden beneath her conical hat, crouching beside a street cart. She was washing a wok out in the water that was running down the gutter. Moira gave whatever was being fried up on the street cart a big fat red cross and carried on until she came to an airy café on the bustling road. *This was more like it.*

She ordered and arranged herself at one of the tables so she could watch the street life. As she did so she caught a darting movement out of the corner of her eye. Swivelling her head, she was just in time to see a fat brown rat scarpering from the kitchen. It skittered across the café floor, out the door, over the pavement, and disappeared down into the deep gutter. Moira wished Mrs Flaherty were here, she'd have made short work of that fella with her rolling pin she thought shuddering. She tried to put the rat out of her head as her steaming coffee arrived, dark and sweetened by condensed milk. It was reviving and she sipped on it trying not to think about whether Roger the Rat was running solo or if he'd left his extended family behind.

A little boy who looked to be around the same age as her nephew shyly inched his way toward her while she waited for her omelette and she smiled, receiving a dimpled grin by return. He was selling chewing gum and postcards. She already had a pack of gum in her pocket and Mammy had bought enough postcards to make a mural when they got home but his brown eyes were looking at her so beseechingly. Sure, she thought even the most cynical of tourists would struggle to say no to that face. She was glad Mammy wasn't here to bear witness to her handing over her money. She could almost hear her saying, 'That's the pot calling the kettle black, so it is, Moira.' It would be fair play to her to given it was only last night she'd told her how hopeless she was at saying no.

She watched him stuff the notes in his shorts pocket before scarpering off, full of energy, and wondered what life had in store for him. He should be at school not hawking his wares to the tourists but then what right did she have to judge. This wasn't her country. Her mind flitted to Noah with his orderly, routine filled, pampered life. How different the two boys' lives must be but she was guessing if you sat them next to each other and rolled a ball over to them they'd soon be kicking it around like the best of mates.

The omelette arrived a moment later and when she looked up again the little boy was gone. She tucked in hitting Roger the Rat away with her imaginary hammer as he kept popping up, only he'd morphed into more of a grinning mole type of a thing like that old arcade game you found at fairs. The omelette was tasty despite Roger's best efforts to put her off but she had to concede there were only so many omelettes a girl could eat. She might have to branch out and try something different. She glanced at the postcard lying face up on the table she'd chosen. It was a glossy picture of a big white Buddha resplendent against a blue sky. She flipped it over, and read *Lon Song Pagoda, Trai Thuy Mountain, Nha Trang*. She wouldn't mind checking that out today, it looked very impressive, but first things first, she fancied a bit of beach time.

Feeling comfortably full and considerably perkier than she had an hour ago, Moira set off again in search of a pharmacy. It didn't take her long to find one and the transaction was surprisingly straightforward. The chemist was well used to tourists and their delicate tummies. His English was good too and he'd suggested she buy a bottle of Coke for her mammy as the sugar and caffeine would help perk her up. She made a pitstop at an internet café, scrolling through the messages. Aisling was checking in to make sure she and Mammy hadn't murdered each other and Andrea's email was annoyingly vague. She banged off quick replies to say that postcards would be on their way and not to worry if they didn't hear from them because she wasn't sure how easy internet access was going to be to find from hereon in. Then armed with her supplies she made her way back to the hotel.

Mammy was in the shower when Moira pushed the door open and she flopped on to the edge of the bed flicking through the guide book to find directions to the White Buddha. It wasn't too far she thought, her finger tracing the route; she could walk it. When Mammy appeared a few minutes later, her swimsuit on beneath her fisherman pants, Moira could see that despite her attempts at brightening herself up she was still pale. There was no way she'd be up to anything strenuous today. It looked like she'd be visiting the pagoda on her own. She handed her the pills and the bottle of Coke and then kicked back on the bed for a bit reading up on the local sights to wait while the fizz and tablets worked their magic.

It was odd, she mused, keeping one eye on the text she was reading and one on the rogue gecko on the ceiling above her; yesterday she'd felt out of sorts because she wasn't baking in the sun sipping cocktails or hanging out at a bar chatting up her fellow backpackers. Today, she wanted to explore. She'd done plenty of hanging out in pubs chatting up the fellas and she could lie out in the sun and bake at home—well at least three times over summer any road! She'd come all this way, and it had just dawned on her she didn't want to waste a moment.

'I'm feeling better now, Moira, that Coke helped thanks. Marvellous stuff the Coca-Cola. I'm not up for a marathon but

I think I could manage a sun lounger in the shade with my book.'

'I'll join you for a while but I wouldn't mind having a wander about.'

THE BEACH WAS A HIVE of industry as hawkers in full force patrolled the waterfront sun loungers, smiling and offering their wares to pink-faced tourists. Moira surveyed the shore until she spotted two free sun loungers off in the distance in the shade of a palm tree. That would do nicely she thought, marching off in that direction. She placed her towel on the spare lounger while Mammy arranged herself on hers. 'Another Coke?'

'Grand.'

Moira returned with a drink for them both and settled herself on her seat. The surf was white and frothy and she lay back listening to it crash along the beach. It was such a soothing sound; she could see why Rosi liked playing those beach music tapes of hers. The whale song she didn't quite get but the sound of the sea was lovely. She lay there until she was good and hot and couldn't face turning down another smiling face offering her a paperback book or tropical fruit, before going for a dip. Mammy, mercifully, was snoozing and hadn't seen the woman with her steaming tin pots of shellfish approach them. Moira had shaken her head vehemently and she'd carried on her way. There must have been some weight in those pots, she thought watching her pad toward a huddle of skimpily clad sunseekers, her shoulders stooped. She plunged straight into the surf and the water cooled her off as she floated around, bobbing with the waves until she'd had enough. It was time to go and explore.

MOIRA FANNED HERSELF with the guidebook and gulped down the cold water she'd bought at the base of the steps. It was so, hot, she could feel the shirt and shorts she'd pulled on over her bikini sticking to her. She gave the guidebook one last wave for good measure, managing to swat a lazy, humming dragonfly away before retrieving her camera from her pack. She crouched down and angled it upwards, overwhelmed by the scale of the Buddha as she craned her neck and tried to fit it in its entirety in the frame. She wouldn't do it justice she knew that; you wouldn't get a feel for the scale of it in a photograph but it would make a stunning picture nonetheless with that brilliant blue sky behind it.

She spied a shady corner in the pagoda and made for that. The climb up all those steps had been worth it she decided as she saw Nha Trang spread out like a roll of carpet below. It was very peaceful up here which surprised her. She'd assumed it would be mobbed like the beach but the only hawkers were in the car park below. Then again, she'd chosen the hottest part of the day to come and visit. She was beginning to fall a little in love with this country, she realised, wiping her face with her shirt sleeve. When was the last time she'd stood somewhere silently and just let the scene wash over her? She was thinking clearly for the first time in a long while too and had stopped being frightened of where her thoughts might take her because standing here now thinking about her daddy it didn't feel like a dark place with no hope.

Moira remembered how he used to sit playing the spoons at the table come teatime. She had no idea why he did that, it was just something he did while they waited for Mammy to put dinner on the table. It always made her smile even when it was fried liver and onions on the menu—*it's full of iron for young girls, Moira*, Mammy would say. She smiled now too recalling how he'd stick the tea cosy on his head when he went to pour from the pot. He was silly her daddy and she loved him for it. He was part of her, *her* story and he always would be.

Her recollections were broken by a tour bus group materialising through the hazy heat waves at the top of the stairs. Their faces peered out from under umbrellas in an attempt to shield the midday sun. It was time to go and check on Mammy, Moira decided.

'JAYSUS, MAMMY! I WAS only gone a couple of hours. What have you done?'

'Don't you like it?' Maureen sat up and swished her hair back and forth, the beads in the tiny woven braids decorating her head clacking.

'Mammy, you look,' Moira was momentarily speechless. 'You look—'

'Like yer Bo Derek in that film, Ten?'

'No, Mammy not Bo Derek. She was blonde, tall, and tanned, not short, Irish and sixty when she starred in that.'

'You're never too old to try a different look I say, Moira, and you'll be wishing you'd had yours done when all I have to do of a morning is rinse and go.' Maureen pointed across the rows of sun loungers that had been filling up the empty sand in Moira's absence. She followed the line of her finger to where a tiny bird-like woman was crouched over a lobster woman, her deft fingers weaving her frizzy blonde hair into cornrows of braids.

'She's no feckin Bo Derek either,' Moira muttered. 'She should know better.'

'I could call her back over when she's finished. Her name's Chau, it mean's like a pearl. Isn't that lovely? She could do yours too if you like, Moira? We'd look like sisters, so we would.'

'Over my dead body, Mammy. One of us looking like they're about to burst into a Boney M song is more than enough.'

'I like a bit of Boney M, especially around Christmas time. And I'll have you know, yer man at the bar over there, him in the scanty pants, has been sniffing around while you've been gone.'

Moira turned toward the beach bar from which the strains of Bob Marley's One Love drifted. She saw a ruddy faced man who was indeed in scanty pants leaning against the bar, a cigarette smouldering in the ashtray beside him. His chest looked as though it had one of those shag pile rugs glued to it and as for the rest, well, she was trying not to look. He caught her staring over and raised his can in greeting.

Mammy elbowed her. 'Don't be after gawping at him or he'll think I'm interested and I don't know how to say feck off in German.'

They looked at each other and burst into a fit of giggles.

Chapter 18

Postcards

Dear Rosi,

The pictures on the front are of Po Nagar Cham Towers, the White Buddha and the Cai River. Cham Towers are really, really old and were used by the Buddhist monks for worship. We visited them as the sun was setting and the stones almost looked like they were on fire. I enjoyed the White Buddha too and the Cai River with all the blue fishing boats was pretty. We've had a grand time in Nha Trang apart from Mammy getting the trots. I've found it very peaceful. There's something about these Buddhist temples that makes me feel calm. I can see why you do yoga and all those breathing exercises. Mammy's on at me not to forget I'm a Catholic but I can't take anything she says seriously at the moment. She's after having her hair braided and looks like a geriatric Irish version of Bo Derek. Honestly, Rosi, you want to see the state of her. If I catch her jogging down the beach in a one-piece then I'm on the next plane home.

Love Moira

DEAR ANDREA,

Have you and Jeremy, you know? I can't be too specific in case the postman is the type who reads people's postcards but you'll know what I'm getting at. I've seen a few rideable men here but I think the fact I'm travelling with my mammy is scaring them away. It seems to be having the opposite effect for Mammy—a German man in his underpants took a shine to her today. Honestly, Andrea, I could hardly see his thing for his belly, not that I was looking! It disturbed me to think of Mammy being chatted up too. I haven't been thinking about Michael too much since we left. I've been focussing my thoughts on Tom, his bum in particular. It's therapeutic. Mammy and I haven't murdered each other yet although once or twice I've been tempted. Vietnam is very hot and sticky but it is surprisingly interesting and we've seen and done a lot since we got here. It's been nice kicking back and enjoying the beach here in Nha Trang but we're moving on again tomorrow to Hoi An. Hope the weather back home is not too shite.

Love Moira

Mammy's Travel Journal

HELLO FROM HOI AN. Well, today was the longest bus ride of my life, thirteen hours we were on that auld rust bucket on wheels and I don't mind telling you there were times I wasn't sure we'd make it here. Moira said she felt like she was engaged in a never-ending game of chicken, what with all the trucks not keeping to their lane. Their constant honking hurt my head. The roads off the motorway were a nightmare too. The tar seal was non-existent in parts and we did more jigging in our seats than yer Michael Flaherty fella in Riverdance. I had to have words with HIM upstairs asking HIM to get us there in one piece.

HE is good, so he is, and here we are but I tell you a lovely thing did happen along the way. I made a new friend. Her name's Sally-Ann and she lives on a sheep farm but not for much longer as she's sold it, not far from a town beginning with K, in Western Australia. I keep thinking it's called Kangaroo but sure, that can't be right. I recognised her from our journey from Hoi Chi Minh to Nha Trang and when I saw her getting on the bus I waved out. She sat down across from me because Moira pinched the window seat again and wouldn't budge. I warmed to her straight away not just because I liked her eyes, they're such an unusual shade of blue but because she said she liked my hair. I wished Moira had heard her say that but she had her headphones on.

Sally-Ann told me to call her Sal because everybody does. We chatted a bit about our homes, hers she said is a dusty, dry place in the summer but that she loves the wide uninterrupted sky and would struggle to live anywhere else. She said she's going to find it hard moving into the town but that it's time and she's looking forward to being a stone's throw from her sister. I told her about O'Mara's and how I've downscaled to an apartment, not a flat mind, I was quick to point that out, near the sea in Howth. It turned out she's a widow too. Her husband died earlier in the year. It was the cancer. I reached across and gave her hand a squeeze when she told me that because she got a little teary and I could see her grief was still raw.

We talked a little about that, how hard it is to find yourself on your own after so many years spent with someone else. Especially, if they were good years. And how some days you just don't want to get out of bed but with your children keeping their beady eyes on you, you somehow manage to. It's a hard thing, Sal said, having to put a brave front on for the sake of your kids. I told her that's just a mammy's lot and she agreed.

It's not the big romantic stuff you miss either, not that my Brian was a flowery sorta man. Although he did buy me a bottle of Arpège on our wedding anniversary, all our married years— never missed. Praise where praise is due, I say. No, it's not the sweeping sentimental gestures on anniversaries or birthdays it's the everyday things. The sitting on the sofa together dunking your biscuit in the cup of tea he's made you. The way he always agrees with you when you moan about some eejit on the television. It's those sorta things and I said to Sal you think your life is going one way and then it picks you up and throws you on your arse. She said that's exactly how it is. Our chat was a good distraction from all those trucks.

She and her husband, Robert, had grand plans of getting someone in to manage their farm in a couple of years so they could be freed up to travel. They fancied Europe because you couldn't find anywhere else more different to the K place she comes from. She told me it was always something they'd planned on doing one day. The thing is we both agreed, 'one day' doesn't always come.

She wanted to see the Leaning Tower of Pisa and her Robert wanted to see the Eiffel Tower. She wasn't much interested in seeing either now. She said her kids talked her into selling up and buying in town where her sister lives. It would give them peace of mind because she couldn't manage on her own and they had no interest in coming home to help run the farm. A farm was a tie, she said, and if she hadn't of done what they wanted and sold up she wouldn't have been able to travel here. It broke her heart to let it go because of all the memories it held, not just her and her husband's but of growing up and her parents too. I told her how it was the memories that made me leave O'Mara's. They were suffocating me. We all handle things differently.

We moved on after that and I asked her what had brought her to Vietnam. She told me she nursed here in the war and that's how she met Robert. She hadn't thought she'd ever come back but he'd wanted her to. He'd made her promise she would because he thought it would help her make peace with the past. She said her kids thought she was mad coming back on her own but they hadn't pushed it too much, not after getting their way with her selling the farm. She was glad she'd come because it was comforting to see that life even after a catastrophic war, carried on. It was hopeful, she said.

She asked why Moira and I had come and I felt a bit funny telling her it was because I've always wanted to sail on a junk after seeing James Bond do it in a film. And, Moira's come with me because she was getting herself in bother at home and needed a break. I mean there's Sal busy saving all those poor people's lives in terrible circumstances and there's me hankering after Roger Moore and making sure my daughter doesn't fall off the wagon.

Moira's moaning on at me to turn the light out as she wants to be up early to have a look around in the morning. I can't believe this is the same girl I left Dublin with; I mean this is Moira. I just about had to put a rocket under her bed to get her up most mornings!

Chapter 19

Sally-Ann inspected her room. It would do just fine she thought, dumping her pack at the foot of the bed. She liked the arrangement the bus company had with the local hotels because she'd been perfectly happy to stay at the first one it had stopped at. Everybody had their hand in somebody's pocket but sometimes that worked and if it meant she didn't have to trawl around a strange town in the dark quibbling over a few dong for a bed then she was all for it. She'd venture out and find something for dinner shortly but first she'd just stretch out for a few minutes, she decided, kicking her shoes off and flopping down on the bed. It was comfortable and she knew after the long journey today she'd sleep like a baby later.

It had been a boon Maureen introducing herself on the bus. Sally-Ann would have smiled at her, recognising her of course from their journey to Nha Trang. She doubted she'd have initiated a conversation though. She was too reserved for that. She'd always been one of life's observers whereas Maureen was an outgoing woman. The kind of woman who'd start a conversation with strangers waiting at the check-out in the supermarket. Or, for that matter, strangers on a bus.

Sally-Ann had warmed to her immediately, and they'd clicked over their common ground. It had been nice talking to someone who understood how she was feeling. She was sure to bump into her and her daughter again given they were staying here in Hoi An at the same hotel and following a similar itinerary north as far as Hue, any road. Their reasons for coming here couldn't have been more different though, she mused, her eyes feeling heavy. The memories of the bloodshed she'd seen here was scored on her brain but there had been good things that had happened here too and that was why Robert had wanted her to come back. He'd hoped she'd find resolution. It was here after all that they'd met and here she'd sat holding little Binh's, whose name ironically meant peace, hand all through the night. It was also here she'd stopped being that wet around the ears girl from Katanning.

Maureen had smelt of Arpège again today. The soft floral fragrance tugged at Sally-Ann's memory and as her lids drooped shut, she found herself remembering a different time.

1967

STREWTH IT WAS HOT, Sally-Ann thought, not for the first time, as she went about her rounds of the ward here at the No.4 Hospital, Butterworth. The beds were filled by a mix of Brits and Gurkhas, the young Nepalese men serving in their brigade of the British Army. Their reputation was that of being fierce fighters, something she found at odds with the gentle natured men she was enjoying looking after.

She could feel her white veil wilting in the heat despite the starching it had received and felt ridiculously overdressed for the infernal heat, it would be the end of her she was sure. Not for the first time she shook her head, the cursed limp material sticking to the back of her neck with the movement. It was

1967 for heaven's sake and she was wearing a veil. Ridiculous, Sally-Ann huffed silently.

Still, she shouldn't complain. What was a bit of discomfort compared to what these poor diggers had been through, were still going through? How strange it was to think that one short year ago her biggest worry had been how to stop Billy Brown and his persistently wandering hands from reaching their end goal. She'd dealt with that pretty swiftly by accidently on purposing upending her drink in his lap, and she'd deal with feeling like she was permanently paddling about in a hot bath too.

Sometimes Sally-Ann had to pinch herself that she wasn't the star of a peculiar dream when she ventured out to explore with her new friend, Margaret, on their day off. The sights and sounds were so different to home and she was soaking up all of those differences. She'd never been on a plane in her life either, until she'd decided to volunteer and then things had happened very quickly. A few signed papers and much wringing of her mum's hands when she'd made the call to tell her what she'd decided to do, and she'd found herself on a Qantas flight bound via Singapore for Malaysia.

The humidity when she'd disembarked had been oppressive and had been unrelenting ever since. She couldn't imagine a time when she'd get used to this cloying tropical climate. The air was so heavy and thick it weighed her down. It made mundane tasks feel like hard work and she was perpetually tired though it wasn't surprising given the long shifts she was rostered on, ten hours at a time six days a week. Now, she stifled a yawn, giving herself the hard word. It was her job to put on a bright and cheery face as she bustled about looking after these boys, who were such a long way from home and some of whom looked like they were barely out of school. She hadn't come here to stand around looking like she was ready for bed!

Oh, but she was finding things tough. So much tougher than she'd expected but then she didn't know what she'd expected, her experience of life outside Katanning being somewhat limited. Not that she admitted any of this when she wrote her weekly letters home. She was upbeat and full of the sights she was seeing, not dwelling on the heart-breaking side of her nursing role. For someone who'd always struggled to keep a secret she was getting adept at keeping things from her family. It wasn't just the heat, it was the unexpected Britishness of her posting that had thrown her off kilter. She'd barely gotten her head around the Australian Army's jargon in the short time since she'd enlisted and been sent to Ingleburn Army Hospital, let alone even attempt to decipher the unfamiliar ranks here at Butterworth.

That cocky girl with her brand new title, Lieutenant Sally-Ann Jessop who'd left Australia four short weeks ago with a certainty that after her practical experience at Ingleburn she was going to be a brand-new shiny asset to the army, had had an awakening as rude as a bucket of cold water being thrown over her upon arrival here at Butterworth.

'How are you today, Liz?' an accent she'd been informed came from the Midlands of England asked. Twinkly blue eyes with sandy lashes peered up at her, the rest of his face hidden beneath a swathe of bandages but the tufts of hair protruding from the top giving away his red-headed genetics.

She'd gotten used to the banter of the soldiers. It was harmless and she'd soon come to realise if they were capable of mustering up a bit of cheek then it should be taken as a positive sign. The spirit of some of the lads after what they'd been through amazed her. They epitomised brave in her opinion. 'That's enough from you, Edward. You know full well its *Sister* to you.' Sally-Ann tutted, the smile she gave him belying the stern tone as she set about checking his bandages. He'd decided her eyes were the colour of Elizabeth Taylor's and had taken to calling her Liz. Not very cheeky on the scale of things. He was only nineteen and he was going home with one leg missing. It broke her heart.

She finished her rounds and with her shift finished, made her way down the corridor heading toward the nurse's quarters. A senior, more experienced nurse, Eileen Wilson, who had an intimidating air about her, one that didn't lend itself to cheeky banter, materialised from one of the wards and called her aside. She steeled herself for a dressing-down unsure what misdemeanour she'd committed but Sister Wilson wasn't one for idle chit-chat.

'I'd like you to assist me on the next medevac flight to Vung Tau, Sister. Do you think you're ready for that?'

'Oh,' she hadn't expected that and she hesitated, momentarily on the back foot, until the impatient question in Sister Wilson's no-nonsense grey eyes galvanised her. 'Yes, Sister, definitely.' Sally-Ann breathed, feeling that urge to pinch herself once more. She would be flying into Vietnam to bring their wounded boys back to the safety of Butterworth until they could be flown home. Her stomach flipped and then flopped with a mixture of fear and excitement at what lay ahead.

'Goodo.'

Sally-Ann was being dismissed and she nodded at Sister Wilson, 'Thank you, Sister,' before continuing on her way.

'Sister Jessop.'

She paused hearing her call after her and turned, 'Yes, Sister?'

'Do you have any perfume here with you?'

It was the strangest of questions Sally-Ann thought as she nodded.

'Wear it, I find it helps.'

SALLY-ANN PUZZLING over what she'd taken to be an order from Sister Wilson, went back to the nurse's quarters. The stuffed koala bear she'd brought with her from home and nicknamed Lily for no reason other than she liked the name, was perched on her pillow and she said, 'Hello, Lily' as she always did before opening the top drawer in the chest next to her bed. Her prized bottle of Arpège was tucked away in there, it being the coolest place she could find to store it. She'd been told or had read somewhere that sunlight and heat were not good for fragrance, they'd change the notes of the perfume.

She opened the drawer to retrieve it, the sight of the black and gold canister instantly conjuring up the memory of her twenty-first birthday. There'd been candles and cake and even a small glass of champagne to celebrate her coming of age, followed by her favourite dinner. Roast lamb with Mum's mint sauce and new potatoes. Afterwards she'd taken Dad's car and driven to the dance in town, allowed for the first time to take Terri who'd reminded her of a skittish lamb in her excitement. The perfume had been a gift from Mum, Dad, and Terri, her first bottle of French fragrance. She was officially a grown woman.

'Off somewhere nice?' Alice a nurse with a cockney twang from London winked at her. Sally-Ann hadn't heard her come in. She thought Alice was very glamorous, one of those girls who always managed to look put together without seeming to make any effort to do so. She even managed to give her nursing uniform a certain joie de vivre, although, she constantly bemoaned the humidity denouncing it as no good for her mane of thick dark hair. She seemed very worldly to Sally-Ann, London a far-off cosmopolitan place she could barely imagine, and Alice with her huge brown eyes and penchant for bold lipsticks, always brought Natalie Wood to mind. She'd loved *Splendor in the Grass*.

'I'm going to Vung Tau with Sister Wilson.'

'Oh, well, good luck.' She looked at her bemused, but Alice was the sort of girl who always had some place to be and with a smile that said she didn't have time to enquire further as to why she was sitting on her bed holding a bottle of perfume, she said 'I'm more of an Estee Lauder girl, myself,' and swished past and out through the doors at the bottom of their dormitory to the gardens beyond.

Sally-Ann took the lid off the bottle and sprayed generously behind each ear and then on her left wrist holding her right against it for a beat. Susan, with whom she'd done her training, had worked on the perfume counter of her local department store before deciding nursing was her vocation and had told her that rubbing your wrists together bruised the fragrance. As the scent teased her nostrils, she closed her eyes. It made her think of twirling skirts at the dances, stolen kisses in the car park outside the dancehall, and lazy Sunday boat rides down the Swan River. She sat there like that for an age waiting for the word that it was time to go.

SISTER WILSON STRODE ahead, her medical kit banging against her thigh, Sally-Ann scurrying behind her to where the hatch of the Hercules yawned open ready for them to board. Her mind whirred as she thought about the dangers ahead. More than fear for herself though, she was frightened of what she would see when they arrived. The diggers they were going to retrieve would be in a bad way, she knew that. It was their job to get them safely back here to Butterworth from where they'd be flown home within the next couple of days. She'd see horrors she'd never be able to un-see. 'You can do this Sally-Ann, you're a nurse. It what's you're trained to do,' she whispered silently before sending up a prayer to ask for the strength she knew she was going to need to help these boys.

'Arpège?' Sister Wilson asked once they were strapped into their seats. The question pulled Sally-Ann from her reverie. She nodded.

'That's my sister Bet's favourite,' Sister Wilson said offering the younger nurse a smile. She could sense the nervous energy coming off her in waves.

The smile softened her somewhat austere features and it emboldened Sally-Ann to ask, 'Sister, why did you suggest I wear perfume?'

'It's for our boys, Sister, so even if their injuries mean they can't see they at least know they're safe when they smell our perfume.'

Chapter 20

Present

Moira was still half asleep and was grateful for the steaming brew that had just been put in front of her. She'd successfully ordered her and Mammy's morning beverage the local way asking for two cà phê sua nongs. It had made her feel a little bit proud and very intrepid when the woman had nodded her understanding straight away. It made for a pleasant change not to have to listen to Mammy ask for two, holding her fingers up invariably the wrong way (Moira had told her more than once she was actually giving the poor restauranteur the fingers), café au lait coffees please. She enunciated this slowly and in a very loud voice as though that would make what she was ordering clearer.

Now she sipped away on the hot sweet drink. They were sitting under the awning outside the restaurant attached to their hotel. Hoi An remained a surprise for them to discover today because they hadn't seen much from the bus last night. It had been dark when they'd finally rumbled into the city. Their driver had done a quick circuit past rows of fluorescent bulb-lit shops with screeds of colourful fabrics for sale, machinists toiling away in the background before veering off down a labyrinth of side streets and depositing them here.

They'd ordered a club sandwich from the restaurant each but had been too tired to venture out, opting instead for another early night. Moira would not be relaying how many early nights she was having on this holiday in any of her postcards home.

She took in their surroundings as curiosity kicked in along with the caffeine. A row of bikes was parked across the street and a few doors up from them a group of men were sitting on upturned crates, noodles dangling from the chopsticks they were expertly handling. Street dogs snuffled around or lay snoozing in doorways. She watched a woman cycle past with a basket full of fresh greens. Nobody, not even the dogs, seemed to be in any hurry.

'Where you from?' A little girl bobbed up from nowhere, her grin wide, revealing baby teeth pearly white against creamy skin as she grinned up at her.

'Ireland,' Moira smiled back at her, her grin infectious, before putting her cup down.

'You buy?' She produced a selection of colourful bracelets.

'No, not today thanks.' She had an armful of the things as it was.

'Can I have Ireland coin? I collect.' She widened her brown eyes to gaze beseechingly up at her.

She was a pro at this Moira thought feeling a tug at her heartstrings. She dutifully retrieved her wallet from her shoulder bag and opened the flap where she'd put the coins she'd been handed back at the airport. Dublin seemed like another world and retrieving the fifty or so pence she had left she handed the money over. She was rewarded with another smile that made her feel happy inside. The child stuffed the coins in her pocket. 'Bye, Ireland,' she shouted haring off down the street, another hotel with more tourists sitting around in the morning sunshine already in her line of sight. Mammy, Moira realised was smirking over the top of her coffee cup.

'Just say 'No' eh, Moira? N.O. isn't that how it went?'

It was the children she struggled with Moira thought simultaneously poking her tongue out at her mammy. Their little faces, so bright and eager were impossible to say no to. It would feel, well it would feel unnatural to ignore them. She could see that little girl wasn't going hungry but she was spending her days trying to make money and not going to school and that made her sad. It wasn't as though she hadn't seen people in need before. At home there were always hunched mounds sitting on pieces of cardboard as you crossed over the Ha'penny Bridge but they weren't children.

Maureen was unaware of the deep thoughts her daughter was having because she'd spied Sally-Ann. She waved over to where she was standing in the foyer and the Australian woman smiled her recognition before heading over to their table. Maureen gestured to the empty seat. 'Come and join us. We've just ordered.'

'Thank you,' Sally-Ann sat down and smiled at them both before offering up an apologetic, 'I'm starving,' as she picked up the menu. 'I'd planned on heading out to find some dinner last night but I fell asleep as soon as my head hit the pillow. That was some bus ride.'

Maureen and Moira nodded their agreement.

'Maureen, I hope you don't mind my asking but that's Arpège you're wearing isn't it?' She looked over the top of the menu.

'It is, it's my favourite. My husband, Brian, used to buy me a bottle on our wedding anniversary. I'm going to treat myself to a big bottle when we go through duty free on our way home.'

'It was my favourite too. It was the first bottle of French perfume I was ever given. My family gave it to me on my twenty-first birthday.' The two women smiled at each other.

Moira observing the exchange was struck by how different they were. There was Mammy with her ridiculous beaded braids and quick dry T-shirt which she'd teamed with her fisherman pants and sandals, and there was Sally-Ann. She reminded Moira of a scout leader, all she needed was a whistle around her neck. She was decked out in a plain T-shirt, knee length khaki shorts and sensible walking shoes. Her hair was a no-nonsense cropped grey and her demeanour was that of a practical capable, woman. It was her eyes that caught your attention, they were quite startling.

'My husband,' Maureen was saying now. 'Well he wasn't my husband back then, he wooed me with a bottle. It was the first French perfume I'd ever owned too.'

'It's special isn't it? That first bottle. It symbolises womanhood, or at least that's how I felt.' Sally-Ann smiled she'd been about to ask Moira what her favourite scent was but the woman who ran the hotel approached with her pen and pad at the ready and the conversation halted.

'Chào buổi sáng,' Sally-Ann smiled looking up. The woman looked pleased and repeated the sentiment before Sally-Ann added, 'I'll have báhn mi hòa mã please.'

Moira had no idea what she'd just said but she'd just put her cà phê sua nongs to shame.

'Sal told me on the bus yesterday that she nursed here during the war, Moira.' Maureen explained in that irritating tone she used when she was 'in the know'.

'Oh.' Moira had seen plenty of films about the war, hadn't everyone? 'That must have been tough.' It sounded lame given what this woman must have seen and done during that time. She was embarrassed that it was all she could come up with in response but was saved by the arrival of her and Mammy's baguettes along with a selection of jams. She chose grape just because she hadn't had it before and peeling back the seal she listened in as the two women chatted about their plans for the day.

Mammy rattled off all the sights they were looking forward to seeing, the wooden Chinese shop houses and the covered Japanese bridge in the ancient town being top of their list.

'I read in my guide book that Hoi An is the tailoring capital of the world.' Sally-Ann's food arrived, eggs sunny side up with a baguette and she thanked the woman before sprinkling a little chilli sauce over her eggs and continuing. 'Apparently there are over three hundred of them in the city. It's a great place to get clothes made to measure especially custom-made suits. Super cheap.'

Moira received a kick under the table and she sent crumbs flying as she protested.

'Did you hear what Sal just said, Moira? You can get clothes made to measure here. That's what they were up to in those shops we saw from the bus last night. Sure, you could get yourself a whole new work wardrobe.'

Moira was surprised Mammy wasn't already up and out of her seat stampeding up the road to where they'd seen the rows and rows of dressmaking shops. The thought of a whole new work wardrobe wasn't inspiring her to get moving, she didn't want to think about work full stop and she carried on eating her jam and bread.

'I thought I'd see about having something made for my daughter's graduation while I'm here. She's at university in Sydney,' Sally-Ann said. 'I'll need something smart for that.'

'Ooh, you've just reminded me.' Maureen's beads clacked as she jiggled in her seat with excitement. 'I could get a dress made for the Yacht Club Christmas dinner. It's quite formal or so I've been told. Did I tell you, I'm learning how to sail, Sal?'

Sal shook her head, dipping her bread in her yolk, 'No, I don't think you did, Maureen.'

'I took it up recently. It's something I always fancied doing but never had the time when we ran the guesthouse.' And with that she was away. Moira tuned out as she prattled on about her painting classes, the politics of the ladies who golfed, and her rambling group. She informed Sally-Ann she'd learned the key to surviving grief was keeping yourself busy. 'Don't give yourself time to fall into that big black hole.' She wagged her baguette at her. 'And talk about how you're feeling don't let it fester, like Moira here was doing.'

Moira scowled at her mammy. Nothing was sacred with her. She switched off again as Mammy began talking about the counsellor she'd gone to see and how she was hoping Moira might use her services when they got home. Ignoring the one-sided chatter she polished her breakfast off and wished Mammy would shut up and finish her food so they could go and see what the city had to offer.

Chapter 21

'Well what do you think? Is the colour me?' Maureen was standing next to a headless mannequin in a figure-hugging Chinese styled blue silk dress. 'This fabric in that style.' She held up the piece of vibrant red silk she'd plucked from the table where they'd been browsing the stacks of sample fabrics and struck a hands-on-hip pose next to the mannequin.

'Jaysus, Mammy, it's very China Beach. Yer boatie men might think you're touting for business,' Moira said.

Sally-Ann who was feeling a little overwhelmed by the selection, choked back a laugh.

'Don't be rude, Moira, it's lovely and bright so it is and sure, who wants to be a wallflower?' Maureen was holding the material tightly to her chest looking ready to play tug-o-war should her daughter try and take it off her. 'What do you think, Sal?'

'I think life is far too short to be a wallflower, Maureen.'

Mammy shot a triumphant look at her daughter before casting around for assistance. Moira sighed. It looked like the red silk would be making an appearance at the Howth Yacht Club's Christmas do.

'Have you seen anything you like, Moira?' Sally-Ann asked.

'Lots. Too much really, I don't know where to start.' She didn't and she wished she had Andrea with her. She'd help her pick just the right fabric and decide on a style. She always took Andrea shopping with her.

'Me either, although I do like the look of this.' Sally-Ann's hand settled proprietorially over a folded bolt of sea-green silk.

'Oh, that's gorgeous. It would really set your eyes off,' Moira encouraged. 'Do you have a style in mind?'

'I'm not sure. Maybe something like this?' She moved over to another headless dummy only this one was wearing a more sedate, and much more age appropriate in Moira's opinion, black dress. It was sleeveless, the cut simple and stylish.

'I like that, you could get a jacket made in the same fabric too.'

'I could, couldn't I.' Sally-Ann's eyes danced and Moira left her and Mammy to be measured up while she decided to see what was on offer next door. The shops were all much of a muchness, she thought, determined to order something. Although this one she saw, looking around and making a mental note to steer Mammy in the opposite direction when she was finished with her order, had an abundance of baggy ethnic pants on display.

'I'VE REALLY ENJOYED today. Thanks for letting me tag along,' Sally-Ann said. The trio were perched on stools outside a street café in the Ancient Town. They were waiting for the bowls of pho, Sally-Ann had insisted they try. The chicken noodle broth with its plump white noodles was a Vietnamese staple and she'd said they'd be doing themselves a disservice if they didn't at least try it. Mammy had been gung-ho, keen to impress her new friend with her worldly palate but Moira had pursed her lips and taken a bit more persuading. She'd kept flashing back to Roger the Rat from Nha Trang. It made her tummy tighten with apprehension. She was outnumbered though and pho it was. What was the worst thing that could happen? It was the wrong way to think because then she flashbacked to the nightmare of the clam-room.

A whiff of lemon grass and something else she couldn't put a name to, wafted past her on a plate and her nose twitched appreciatively. Maybe it would be alright after all.

'Not a bother. It was a grand day,' Maureen said. 'Wasn't it, Moira?'

'A grand day, Mammy.' She grinned at Sally-Ann.

It had been too. They'd spent an industrious morning trawling the tailors' shops and buying up large. Moira was going to have to be on her best behaviour where Mammy was concerned and not make any more cracks about the red silk—as hard as that would be. She'd no room in her backpack to cart home today's haul and was reliant on Mammy unless she wanted to pay for excess baggage. For someone who'd started off looking about the shops reticently she was now the proud owner, or would be tomorrow when the garments were ready to be collected, two new dresses, a pair of black trousers, and three new tops. She'd thought about ordering Andrea something because they were more or less the same size but then she remembered the way she'd sniggered at Moira going on her hols with Mammy and changed her mind.

She'd also bartered her way into buying three lanterns, in purple, pink, and red, on their way here for dinner too. Mammy had huffed at the lantern purchases saying they'd look ridiculous in the bedroom of a Georgian manor house. Moira had told her that it was debatable whether a Chinese styled dress in red silk would look at home mingling with the stuffy yachting set. They'd begged to differ not wanting to squabble in front of their new friend.

The street they were sitting on was illuminated by lanterns strung across the cobbled lane. If Moira closed her eyes, she could imagine how it would have been when the Japanese, Chinese, and European merchants were here pedalling their wares. The lanterns had looked pretty by day but now, lighting up an inky sky, they were positively magical. They'd all agreed there was something very special about this place. There'd been photo opportunities around every corner and she'd soon whipped through a whole roll of film, looking on enviously at those travellers with up to the minute gear and the new digital cameras that were starting to make an appearance.

The first of the fragrant bowls of soup arrived and Sally-Ann indicated Moira should have it. She inhaled the aroma and decided so far so good, then, with all eyes on her she wielded the chopsticks to the best of her ability and fished out a fat white noodle. She slurped it up, feeling it flick against her chin before she caught the rest of it in her mouth. She took a moment to savour it and then looking up gave Sally-Ann the thumbs up.

Postcards

DEAR AISLING,

The picture on the front is of the Japanese covered bridge in Hoi An. The old town here is beautiful. Mammy and her new friend, Sal, and I explored the Chinese quarter which was very quaint with ornate architecture (pinched that description from travel guide book). I loved the lanterns hanging everywhere and I liked the sampan boats on the waterfront too. I used a whole roll of film up just wandering around. You'd love it here because it's got these amazing tailors' shops where you can get clothes made to measure and yes, there were shoes for sale too, lots of shoes. I'm after getting some lovely things made up. To give you a heads-up, Mammy has had a dress made in red silk, think yer red-headed, prostitute woman in China Beach but with Bo Derek braids. She's also had one made for you in blue, and purple for Rosi. I tried to talk her out of it but you know what she's like when she's got her heart set on something. I can't wait to see the three of you in them though. Laughing already.

Love Moira

Dear Roisin

It's your Mammy here. Hoi An is very good value and we've had a grand time. We especially enjoyed looking around the old town. It's another world, so it is. We visited a Chinese merchant house called Tan Ky House. It was very dark and atmospheric with lots of lovely antiques. After that my new friend, Sal, Moira, and I shopped until we dropped. You know those Faraway Tree stories you used to love? Well, if this place was a land at the top of the tree it would be the land of get whatever clothes you want made. How it works is you choose the fabric and the tailor takes your measurements and you're away. I've had a dress made for the Howth Yacht Club's Christmas Dinner in red silk. It's very elegant. Moira suggested I get dresses made in the same style for you and Aisling. You can't afford to put any weight on because I used Moira's measurements. I think you girls will love them, they're both in your colours.

Love Mammy

Dear Noah,

It's your nana here. We are in Hoi An. It is very nice here with lots of shops with colourful things for sale. Your Aunty Moira has bought lanterns like the big white paper shade you have in your bedroom except hers are made of material and are the sorta colours that would keep you wide awake at night not send you off to sleep. The streets here are decorated with them and a long time ago Hoi An was a port town and people came from Japan and China to sell things. I had a soup called pho which had noodles as fat as worms in it. It was very tasty. I hope you're being a good boy for your mammy and dad give them a hug from me and have one for yourself.

Love Nana

Chapter 22

Mammy's Travel Journal

Hello from Hue where we have just had a very interesting meal of rice paper rolls stuffed with pork and I'm not sure what else but it was tasty and very good value. The rolls were Sal's suggestion, she knows her way around a Vietnamese menu, so she does. I liked them but Moira said the texture reminded her of a— well, I knew what she was going to say and it wasn't appropriate for sharing around the dinner table. I kicked her under the table before she had the chance to say the word. Sal doesn't need to hear my daughter's uncultured response to rice paper rolls and for the record there was nothing rubbery about the rolls whatsoever.

I was sad to leave Hoi An but the drive here through the Hai Van Pass was very beautiful. I could have been excused for thinking I was in County Clare what with all the greenery, spitty rain, and rainbows. It was more jungle-like than Clare though and we had magnificent views down to crescent shaped white sand beaches. They don't have those in Clare either. I was worried for a while there that history would repeat itself with Moira. She's not good on the winding roads and I had a paper bag at the ready but Sal came to the rescue. She gave her a ginger sweet to suck on and it did the trick.

Sal was very quiet on the journey here. I did ask if everything was alright and she said she was fine, just a little lost in the past which is understandable. Although as I always say, it doesn't

*pay to bottle things up. I'll be sad to go our separate ways but
we travel up to Hanoi from here and she's going to visit some
unpronounceable village in the hills. I'm not sure why. She didn't
say and as much as I'd have liked to have prodded for more
information there was something in her face that stopped me from
prying.*

*This morning we were up bright and early and I have to say
the cooler weather here was a shock to the system but I'd come
prepared. I have one long sleeved quick dry top; it's got a little
pocket on the front and I think the orange looks well on me. I'm
very impressed with the versatility of my travel pants. I can zip
them off at the knees and wear them as shorts in the hot weather,
then zip them back on in the cool, like I did this morning. I think
Moira was secretly impressed especially as it means I didn't have
to pack all manner of shorts and trousers. I had plenty of room in
my pack when we left Dublin but the way she's been going we're
going to have to buy an extra bag to cart all the gear home. Moira's
turned into a bit of a haggle monster; she loves it so she does. The
thrill of bartering.*

*Sal announced she needed to organise how she was going to
get to this village she's set on visiting after breakfast so we arranged
to do our own thing for the day. We agreed to meet up later for
dinner and went our separate ways. Moira and I set off to visit the
Forbidden City first. Doesn't that just sound delicious? We agreed
it made us feel like we were visiting somewhere very cutting edge
you know like Eastern Germany or the likes when the wall came
down. I remember watching that on the news and feeling all sorta
fizzy inside.*

*Inside the city walls it was a ruin but the Imperial Palace has
been restored. Splendid is the word that comes to mind. Splendid*

and opulent, but sure, that's two words. We headed back to town after that and wandered down to the Perfume River, isn't that a lovely name for a river? I don't know how they came up with it because it was brown like the Mekong. I was impressed by Moira's negotiating skills as she organised for us to go by dragon boat to the track that would lead us to Tu Duc's Royal Mausoleum. The boat was home to yer man steering us down the river, his wife, and five children. No privacy in their household. I had to wonder how they get on. I mean I was mortified the time Patrick had a bad dream and barged in on me and Brian engaged in the, you know what.

It was very relaxing sitting on that boat watching the world go by. We saw people working in the fields, children riding on buffalos with kites flying behind them, and women washing their clothes in the river. Sure, you wouldn't want to be doing your whites in that water. We were on the boat about an hour before we docked. It was a four kilometre hike to the mausoleum and from what we could see it looked very muddy. Moira looked at me and I looked at Moira and we both looked at the man with the scooters for hire. We made a pact, that neither of us would tell Aisling.

Moira drove the thing and I sat on the back and we were grand until she got cocky and wasn't looking where she was going. She rode right through a puddle and we got covered in mud. She really is ruing the day she didn't invest in some quick dry gear now.

Yer man Tu Duc was a one. We read in our guide book that he was only 153cm tall. He had 104 wives and countless concubines. I said to Moira he was suffering badly from the short man's disease. The funny thing is he went to all this trouble to have the tomb built and then he wasn't even buried there. No one knows where he wound up buried along with all his treasure because the two hundred servants who put him in the ground all had their heads cut off to keep it a secret from grave robbers. Charming, he obviously didn't believe in rewarding loyal service.

Chapter 23

Moira was making short shrift of her breakfast as Mammy and Sally-Ann nattered on in between bites. She was only half listening but her ears pricked up when she sensed their conversation was about to get interesting.

'So, come on then, Sal, tell us about this village you're off to.' Maureen had decided there was nothing else for it, she'd have to pry. It was obvious Sal wasn't going to be forthcoming without a nudge. Sometimes in life people needed a good nudge.

'It's a long story.'

'Ah sure, we're not in a rush to head off are we, Moira?'

Moira looked up from her eggs. 'No, no rush.' She was curious to hear what Sally-Ann had to say. It was a bit weird her going off on her own to some village out in the middle of nowhere.

Sally-Ann looked from one to the other. They'd think her mad if she told them. Then again maybe she was. What was the saying? A problem shared is a problem solved was that it? Or was it a problem halved? Well, either way they wouldn't be able to solve this for her but perhaps talking about why she'd come all this way might help to make some sense of it. She took a deep breath and put her knife and fork down.

1968

SALLY-ANN WAS MORE tired than she'd ever been in her life. She now understood what it meant when people said they were 'bone tired'. Her bones did indeed ache with weariness. There were days she was sure her body was fuelled by adrenalin and not much else. She'd just come off a ten-hour shift, the sixth in a row here at the Vung Tau 1st Australian Field Hospital and her plan was to sleep, sleep, and sleep! Maybe tomorrow she'd see if she could borrow Lynn's tape recorder and microphone instead of putting pen to paper. She owed them a letter back home.

She felt the familiar pang for home. Terri had herself a young man now and from the last few letters her sister had written to her, she was in those heady throes of first love. She was describing things in greater detail as though all her senses had suddenly come to life. There was an underlying joy to her words that made Sally-Ann wistful; it wasn't something she'd ever experienced. You could hardly count Billy Brown and his wandering hands as a grand passion. Terri and Terry though, she shook her head and smiled, you wouldn't read about it. She couldn't have met a Henry or a John she had to meet a Terry. One of them would have to revert to their full name. Teresa had always been Terri though and as for Terry she had no clue whether he'd answer to Terence. It must drive their friends mad!

It would be nice to be lying on her bed at home as Terri chattered on. To be hearing first-hand about her life. She missed her but she steeled her resolve as she always did when the homesickness tugged. She was needed here. Terri was perfectly happy and one day, before too long, this awful war would be over and she'd be back home probably shaking her head over the ups and downs of her sister's new romance.

She kicked off her shoes and collapsed on her cot not bothering to get out of her uniform. Her own senses had gone into overdrive when she'd first been deployed into this dirty, dusty, chaotic place. She'd spent the last three months assisting on the medevac flights having proved herself more than capable to Eileen as she'd come to call Sister Wilson. It was a process she'd grown comfortable with despite the dangers and even though she was familiar with Vung Tau, a port city, this latest three-month deployment had tried her. She was one month in and being tested to her very limits.

The hospital was tucked away by the beach behind the sand dunes but it was no holiday camp you'd ever want to come and stay at. The South China Sea seemed a pale, washed out version of the beaches from home and even the sand had an ashen tinge. Rubbish choked the gully ways and the lack of sanitation and stink of the place had been a slap in the face for this girl from Western Australia. Their base had been positioned strategically so that the Aussie diggers battling it out nearby were only thirty minutes away from medical care which meant their chances of surviving the horrors they were enduing was far greater. They were horrors Sally-Ann had seen first-hand.

The bloodshed on both sides was like a never-ending newsreel of carnage. Young bodies destroyed, and for what? It was a question she couldn't find an answer for and so she'd stopped asking it.

The shrilling siren penetrated her fug competing with the familiar beating whir of a chopper coming into land. She forced herself into consciousness before staggering down to triage to see how bad it was. The doors slammed open and the stretchers were carried in. The team of nurses on duty swung in to their well-honed routines cutting the wounded men's clothes off to check them over as the medics inserted drips. Sally-Ann rolled up her sleeves and set to work. She didn't know how many hours had passed before she saw the local boy lying on a gurney in the far corner of the resuscitation area. He stared back at her with glassy eyes.

'Poor kid, an orphan, I think. He was brought in on a rickshaw before this kicked off. He's lost his leg from the knee down.' Sister Healey had followed Sally-Ann's gaze.

'A landmine?'

'Mm.'

'Jesus, he can't be more than ten years old.' It wasn't anything Sally-Ann hadn't seen before but there was something in this boy's eyes as they'd locked on hers. They seemed to be pleading with her. She knew too, the day she failed to be shocked that people could do this to one another was the day she had to go home.

'You're rostered off, aren't you?'

'Yes.'

'Go then, get some rest. We can manage now.'

She looked over at the boy once more and felt herself being pulled over as she realised what else she'd seen in those desperate eyes. It was fear. She smiled reassuringly at him as she took his hand in hers holding it gently. He gripped hers back. 'My name's Sally-Ann, what's yours?'

He looked at her blankly for a moment but then seemed to register what she'd said. 'Sally-Ann?' he said in heavily accented English.

'Sally-Ann, but you can call me Sal.'

She thought she saw the faintest of smiles. 'Binh.'

'Well, I'm here now, Binh. You're going to be okay because I'm going to watch over you.' He squeezed her hand tightly in understanding.

'You stay?'

'I won't leave you, I promise. I'm staying right here. Now try and sleep,' she said pulling up a chair to sit alongside him, listening as his breathing began to slow and calm as he drifted off to sleep. Sally-Ann fell asleep in her chair, her body hunched over with her head resting on the side of the bed and she was still there holding his hand when Binh next opened his eyes.

'IRONICALLY THE NAME Binh means peaceful.' Sally-Ann finished her story and Mammy and Moira both blinked as they came back to the present. 'To cut a long story short I received a letter from Binh not long after my husband, Robert, first got ill. It was completely out of the blue, I never expected to hear from him again. He'd sent it to the Royal Australian Army Nursing Corps who'd forwarded it to me. All he wanted, he said in it, was to let me know he was okay and he had a good life. He said he'd never forgotten me. The nurse with the blue eyes who stayed with him.' Her eyes shone suspiciously bright and she blinked several times before carrying on. 'I told you he was orphaned?'

Maureen and Moira nodded; they were entranced.

'Well it turns out Binh was part of Operation Babylift.' She registered their blank faces. 'The US government's response to South Vietnam's pleas to the United Nations and other humanitarian organisations was to put money into airlifting orphans out of Vietnam. There were nearly three thousand babies and children in total who were flown to the US, Canada, Europe, and Australia to be adopted by families eager to help. It wasn't without controversy though because some of the children were taken from poor families who thought they'd be returned to them. And, of course it wasn't easy for these children growing up either. Some were subject to racism and felt they were neither one nor the other, not Vietnamese or American, Australian, Canadian or wherever they'd found themselves transplanted to.'

Maureen made a choking sound; the world was full of sad stories and sometimes the lines blurred between good intentions and what was right and what was wrong. There were no simple fixes when it came to human life. Sure, she'd read enough in the papers at home over the years to understand that. There'd been some terrible things done under her church's watch but they'd been done with the conviction that what they were doing was right. Just because you believed you were doing the right thing didn't always make it so, though. Moira simply shook her head.

'Binh was taken to Canada where he received rehabilitation treatment to learn how to manage the loss of his lower leg. He was adopted by a family with two older sons and he wrote he'd had a happy upbringing with them. He'd always told them he wanted to go back to Vietnam one day though.

It had never stopped being home, as much as he loved his new family. I think perhaps he was lucky, his mother and father must have loved him very much to agree to let him go and he said in his letter that they come and visit him often here in Vietnam.

He finished university in Canada and just as he'd said he would, he came back here. He decided to travel first wanting to see his country and he met his wife on his journey. They settled in Hanoi and four years ago with three children now, they decided they'd had enough of city life. They moved back to the village where she came from and built their farm-stay accommodation with a dream of being self-sufficient. He said they're extremely happy and that it was important to him that I know that because he'd never forgotten me and the kindness I showed him.' Sally-Ann's voice cracked. 'Sorry.' She chewed her bottom lip blinking back the tears that had returned. 'It's just he'd written in that letter that he'd wanted to die that night. He'd lost everything but that I brought him back.'

'Don't be sorry,' Mammy was swiping at her own eyes and the two women exchanged a watery smile. 'It's a wonderful thing you did.'

'I did what any nurse would do. Robert, my husband made me promise before he died that I'd come back to Vietnam and visit Binh. He said I needed to see for myself that he's happy and that the country has moved on. He thought it would bring me some closure.' She shrugged, 'It never leaves you, you see. I mean they have a fancy name for it now PTSD.'

'What's that?' The term tickled Maureen's memory cogs but she couldn't recall what it stood for.

'Post-traumatic stress disorder. When I came home to Australia it wasn't a diagnosable condition. We weren't allowed to talk about our experiences, we just had to go back to our lives as though the war had never happened.'

'See, Moira, bottling it up, it doesn't do anyone any good.'

Sally-Ann fixed those piercing eyes on her. 'She's right, dear, it doesn't.'

This wasn't about her though, Moira thought. She'd been enthralled listening to Sally-Ann and she was seeing the woman sitting across from her very differently. She wasn't Mammy's rather staid looking new friend, sure she was an angel.

'You were his angel, so you were,' Mammy said to Sally-Ann and Moira looked at her in surprise that they'd been thinking the exact same thing.

'No not an angel, just a human being,' Sally-Ann said, but what she said next took them both by surprise.

Chapter 24

'Come with me.' Sally-Ann's piercing gaze swung imploringly from mother to daughter. The idea of these two Irish women she might not have known long, but whom she liked immensely, accompanying her had just occurred to her. She seized hold of it ferociously, surprised by how much she wanted them to join her. She was anxious, she realised, as to how she'd be received. It was one thing to write and tell a woman who'd sat with you through a long night over thirty years ago that your life had turned out well. It was quite another for that woman to turn up on your doorstep to see for herself.

Binh's letter had brought the war crashing back because for so many years it was his face that had haunted her dreams. He'd become her poster boy, that terrified little boy who'd lost both his parents and whose body had been brutally maimed in a fight that wasn't his. It wasn't hers either but she wouldn't have changed her time at Vung Tau. Those men, boys really, and the locals whose lives were in unimaginable turmoil had needed her and the other women she'd worked alongside. She'd grown to love her fellow Sisters as much as she loved Terri. She knew they'd agree too; it had been a privilege to nurse in Vung Tau.

Then, there was the fact she might never have met the digger who'd lost the sight in one eye and whose leg the medic had only just managed to save. Despite his wounds he'd still mustered up a cheeky grin as he asked her if his crown jewels had survived the mortar attack. They'd formed a friendship during his stay in the hospital. A friendship that had developed into something more. She and Robert had married six months after she arrived home. She'd gone back to nursing and he'd taken over the running of her family sheep farm with Mum and Dad happy to pass the mantle and take things easier. Together, they'd built themselves a good life.

Robert had known her better than she knew herself and he'd been right. It was time she put what had happened here to bed. Life could be fleeting or, if you were lucky, it could be filled with stages. She'd been lucky and for Robert's sake as much as her own she needed to embrace whatever this next stage would bring. In order to do that she needed to see Binh with her own eyes.

She realised Moira and Maureen were looking a little taken aback by the insistence in her tone and she flushed, feeling foolish. She barely knew them after all but she couldn't seem to stop herself. "I looked it up on the internet, Mui Ha the village where they live. It's about a two-and-a-half-hour drive from Hue and sits on a popular backpacking trail for those heading further into the mountains.'

Moira could feel a tingling excitement. There was nothing to stop them going with her, they weren't on any fixed itinerary. Maureen however was less certain. 'Ah, but sure, we wouldn't want to be intruding. It's a pilgrimage of sorts you're undertaking. A personal thing.'

'Yes,' Sally-Ann said slowly. 'It is. But to tell you the truth I'm a little scared. I never replied to Binh's letter. He doesn't even know I got it for certain. I booked my flight to Hoi Chi Minh on the spur of the moment and I didn't think about what

I was going to do until I got here. I went down south initially. I needed to lay old ghosts to rest in Vung Tau.' She closed her eyes for a moment. She'd visited the Martyr's Memorial taking her life in her hands as she'd weaved across the busy road to the enormous roundabout in front of the Pullman Hotel. The city was unrecognisable to the one in which she'd lived and worked. Life, however brutally interrupted, never stood still, she'd thought, sitting on a bench and finally letting the memories of her time here wash over her. The good, the bad, and the ugly.

She opened her eyes. 'Vung Tau was nothing like I remembered but I paid my respects and came back to Hoi Chi Minh where I bought a hop on, hop off bus ticket. I'd decided to work my way here to Hue having a look at the country along the way. I thought it would all become clear to me what I was going to do once I got here but I'm no more certain now that I'm doing the right thing by landing on him out of the blue than I was when I bought my ticket.' She shrugged, 'I keep thinking I've been foolish. I should have written back to him, waited for a reply but the thing is, I've made it this far now. I can't leave without seeing him. So, you see you'd be doing me a favour by coming with me. Strength in numbers and all that.'

'Mammy?' Moira looked at her expectantly. She wanted to go. Sally-Ann's story had moved her. 'She needs us.'

Maureen leaned over and rested her hand on top of Sally-Ann's, just like the Australian Nurse had Binh's all those years ago. 'Of course we'll come with you, Sal. It would be an honour, so it would.'

Chapter 25

Moira was sat in the front of the minivan on account of her car sickness tendencies and Maureen and Sally-Ann were strapped into their seats behind her. They were driving through an area lush with leafy green tea plantations and the road was quiet except for the odd motorbike passing them. It was a different pace altogether to what they'd grown used to in the bigger towns and cities. Their driver, Danh, was a jovial sort with a gold tooth which he flashed every time he grinned. He was armed with a toothpick which he used sporadically, steering with one hand when he felt the urge to dig around. Moira looked out the side window when he did this, partly because she didn't want to see what he'd unearth, but mostly because she couldn't bear watching him drive fast enough to leave a cloud of dust behind them down roads that were barely sealed with only one hand. She felt a tap on her shoulder and turning to look found a bag of ginger sweets being waved under her nose.

'Oh, thanks,' she said, helping herself and unwrapping a sweet. She sucked away on it wondering how they'd be received when they got to where they were going. Would this Binh fella know Sally-Ann on sight? It had been over thirty years since they'd met and given the circumstances it was amazing he could recall the nurse who'd stayed with him all through what must have been a horrific night at all. Her kindness above any call of duty had obviously had a profound effect on him.

Sal was a very strong sort of a person, Moira thought, in all senses of the word. Mammy didn't look strong physically but she was fierce on the inside too she'd come to realise. They were both brave women in different ways.

It must be nice to have a vocation, a calling to do something worthwhile, she mused, feeling her kidneys or something like hit the top of her rib cage as they hit a particularly deep pothole and bounced out the other side. Nursing was definitely that, sure it wasn't the sort of thing you decided to do just because you were fed up with being told what to do all the time at school. Her mind drifted to the children she'd seen here. Delightful faces that never stopped smiling flashed in front of her. Their world, while beautiful, was narrow and little would be handed to them along the way. They'd have to fight hard for everything that came their way. To break any moulds would be a battle.

She could have done anything she wanted when she left school. She was lucky but that luck wasn't down to anything she'd done. She hadn't earned the right to have a wealth of opportunities available to her, it was simply down to the circumstances of her birth. And what had she done with all those endless possibilities? She thought of Mason Price and frowned. There was nothing wrong with her job. It was a good job, a respectable job, and it paid well but it wasn't a calling or a vocation at least not for her. It wasn't, if she were honest with herself, what she wanted to do.

She'd never admitted that before and she shifted in her seat aware of a restlessness building. It was a restlessness that had been gnawing at her for a while now but she hadn't known what it was about and she'd put it aside upon arriving here. The question she'd been unable to face was staring her right in the face. If she didn't see herself at Mason Price then where did she see herself?

Danh honked his horn shooing her confusion away and a cluster of children, their school bags dangling from small shoulders, waved out. Moira smiled and waved back as enthusiastically, seeing their beaming faces as they jostled to be noticed. A beat later a bike went past and she did a double-take. 'Did you see that?'

Danh laughed. 'No big deal.'

She craned her neck to see Mammy and Sally-Ann. 'There was a man and a woman on that scooter with a live pig squashed between them.'

Mammy peered behind to see if she could see them but they were gone and besides she wouldn't have seen much through the brown dust anyway.

'I once saw a calf being transported on one,' Sally-Ann smiled at the memory.

'Mui Ha, not far now,' Danh announced, and true to his words it wasn't long before they began to see more signs of life in the rice paddies on either side of them where workers laboured. The gates denoting the entrance to a village appeared ahead of them and Danh slowed. They were elaborately adorned with Vietnamese script along the top of the bricked arch and down either side. The leaves of a gnarled tree grazed the windows as they passed through them. 'Banyan tree, very old. It's traditional in Vietnamese village. It watches the good times and bad times of the peoples,' Danh explained. 'Mui Ha famous for carpentry and grapefruit. Very good.'

Moira assumed he meant both were very good. She could already see it wasn't the blink and you'd miss it village she'd envisaged but rather a sizable place and as they wound into its heart, she saw numerous alleyways spidering off. They were filled with houses packed tightly together in the same brick as the gates and clad with the weathered clay tiles of the north. A woman cycled past and without the incessant roaring motorbikes it felt relaxed and laid back although the street was bustling with activity. There were several tourists meandering down the main drag pausing to inspect the impressive wood carvings on display. Moira watched a young couple unloading backpacks from the back of a flatbed truck. A food market appeared ahead and Sally-Ann leaned forward and passed across a piece of paper on which she had written Binh's address.

Danh pulled over and wound his window down to call out to a man unloading a container of ripe golden grapefruit. They spoke to one another in rapid fire Vietnamese and then with a nod, signifying he was satisfied he knew where he was going, he wound the window up once more before veering out onto the road.

Moira could sense without seeing Sally-Ann's growing tension as they grew closer. It was palpable and she would have liked to have reached over and held her hand but she wasn't a contortionist. She'd put money on Mammy doing exactly that right now though.

The denser living of the village gave way to the neatly gridded rice paddies once more, the verdant hills a backdrop. It was only a few minutes before Danh slowed once more at the entrance to a driveway. A wooden handmade sign announced they'd arrived at Ben Trang farm. They turned in and parked in an open area where a couple of motorcycles had been abandoned. A house was just visible through the green growth, almost hidden alongside a row of banana trees. Sally-Ann leaned forward tapping Danh on the shoulder. 'Do you mind waiting here with our bags while we go and see whether they have room for us? I didn't book ahead you see.'

'No problem.' He flashed his gold tooth at them all and fished out a packet of cigarettes.

He was probably gasping for one, Moira thought clambering out and inhaling the hint of citrus floating on the breeze.

The trio made their way toward the path leading to the house as a dog, so hairy its eyes were barely discernible, ambled out to greet them, tail wagging with the lethargy of age. Moira stopped to pat him briefly, 'Hello, boy,' she said before scurrying to catch up with Mammy and Sally-Ann. The door to the house was open and the area they ventured into was clearly a reception room. The space was cool, and dark from the shade afforded by the foliage outside. A fish tank gurgled away beside the desk upon which a book lay open with handwritten entries. The sound of a television or radio could be heard emanating from deeper in the house. There was also a cacophonous chattering of birds but it wasn't clear where that was coming from.

'Hello!' Sally-Ann called above the din. They all listened out for movement even though it was unlikely they'd hear a thing over the birds.

Moira realised her own stomach had begun to do flip-flops; how must Sally-Ann be feeling? She glanced over at

Mammy who gave her a funny sort of a smile that told her she was anxious too.

Sally-Ann didn't have to call out twice because a sweet-faced woman who made Moira and Maureen seem tall appeared from where they'd just come. She was carrying an empty dish. 'Sorry, I just feeding the birds. Welcome to Ben Trang farm,' she said, nodding at them as she went to stand on the other side of the desk. She placed the dish down next to the book and picked up a pencil before smiling expectantly up at them. Her English was good.

'We don't have a reservation.' Sally-Ann explained. 'But we would like to stay. First though we wondered if Binh might be here? I'd like to say hello to him.' She spoke slowly and clearly but she didn't shout like Mammy was prone to do, Moira thought, knowing if she were a nail biter, she'd be making short shrift of all ten of them about now. 'I knew him a long time ago.' Sally-Ann left the words 'in the war' hanging.

'He's my husband.' The woman nodded her smile never faltering although a flicker of curiosity was clearly visible on her face. 'Yes, one moment, I go get him.'

Sally-Ann was feeling sick with apprehension. Was she doing the right thing? Would seeing her again conjure up the horror of what had happened to him as a child? Perhaps she was being selfish by coming here. She was trying to help herself after all. What benefit was it to him to have her materialise here at the home he'd built for himself and his family. To distract herself she stepped outside looking around at their surroundings.

The farm she'd seen from their approach down the road was surrounded on one side by pancake flat rice paddies and on the other an orchard of what she was guessing were grapefruit trees. From where she was standing now, a path stretched away from the house and she followed it with her eyes. It snaked around a large pond to a row of bungalows. They were very rustic looking and each had a veranda yawning out over the pond with a hammock on which to while away the day if one so wished. Tucked away down the side of the house was an aviary; the birds it housed still in full conversation. To her right Sally-Ann could see an area fenced off by chicken wire, on the other side of which hens bossed each other about. Beyond that there was a large patch of green which she guessed was a vegetable patch. Behind her, just inside the entranceway, was a bike rack with several ramshackle bicycles. She gazed at them for a few beats unable to remember the last time she'd ridden one of those before turning back, thinking she'd head back inside.

A man had appeared on the path ahead, he walked with a slight awkwardness that was only really detectable if you were looking for it. The woman they'd just met was beside him. Sally-Ann's legs took on a life of their own as, just like they had all those years ago, they propelled her toward him.

Chapter 26

Moira and Maureen had stepped outside and they hung back watching as Sally-Ann drew level with the man. They couldn't see her face but they could see his as he peered at her from beneath the brim of his hat. He frowned for a moment and then as he looked closely at her, his face erupted into a wide incredulous grin. It was as though the sun had come out and both women found themselves exhaling. He held out his arms and Sally-Ann stepped into the embrace. They made a strange pairing, her being a head taller than him. They stayed locked together for the longest time while his wife stood to one side clueless but her smile said she understood that whatever it was that was happening, it was something good. Mammy nudged Moira and she took the tissue she was proffering gratefully, unaware that the tears were running down her face until she tasted their saltiness on her lips.

Less than five minutes later introductions were underway as Sally-Ann half crying and half laughing introduced Moira and Maureen to Binh and his wife, Hoa. Their three children had also appeared wanting to see what the fuss was all about and Binh had hugged them to him providing his mystified family with an explanation as to who Sally-Ann and her friends were. Hoa was holding Sally-Ann's hand tightly as though frightened she might evaporate, her face a picture of wonder.

Now, Sally-Ann, Maureen, and Moira were sitting in Binh and Hoa's living area on a long, low wooden bench seat, which

Maureen was not entirely sure she'd be able to get up from without assistance. Moira had been charged with settling the fare with Danh and telling him that they wouldn't be needing a ride back to Hue. He didn't mind, he'd been paid for a return fare and gracing her with one last flash of gold he ground his cigarette out and got back behind the wheel. Binh was seated across from the three women and Hoa was knelt on a woven mat, upon which stood a dark wooden table separating the group, pouring tea. She kept looking up and smiling at Sally-Ann beatifically. The couple's three children, who ranged in age from fourteen to five, were also kneeling on the mat, chocolate eyes wide, and as quiet as mice lest they miss any of the unfolding story.

'I recognised Sally-Ann's eyes straight away,' Binh said now, his voice still holding traces of his Canadian upbringing. 'So blue. I'd never seen eyes that colour before and I never forgot them, they were so kind. It seemed to me that compassion radiated from them. Eyes never change. You can see a person's soul through their eyes.'

'Unlike the rest of me.' Sally-Ann laughed, her body language relaxed as she accepted the tea from Hoa with a smiling thanks. She told the family about her life in Australia. How she'd married an Australian soldier and that she'd returned to nursing in Australia while he ran the sheep farm they'd bought from her parents. They'd had two children who were now grown-up and had left the family fold for the delights of big city life. She told them how her time in Vietnam had haunted her for many years and how she'd often wondered what had become of Binh. She spoke of her wonder at receiving his letter and how happy it had made her to know he was happy. She explained that it was Robert, her husband, who'd insisted she come back to Vietnam to see him.

Binh reached across the table and took both her hands in his. He looked at her intently as he said, 'I think your Robert must have been a very wise man. And I'm very happy you are here.'

'He was,' Sally-Ann agreed, trying to hold back those pesky tears. This was a happy reunion there would be no more tears.

MOIRA AND MAUREEN HELPED tidy away the remains of the meal. For unexpected guests they had been treated to a feast and were feeling full and more than a little sleepy when Hoa gestured they should follow her. They left Sally-Ann and Binh talking and followed their diminutive hostess through the reception area where she paused to pick up a torch. The glow from the front room illuminated the bicycles lined up in the rack. 'These are for our guests; you are very welcome to make use of them tomorrow.'

Both women murmured their thanks. Moira thought it might be fun to cycle into the village tomorrow for a look around. Mind, she'd seen the hammocks on the verandas of the bungalows earlier when they'd arrived. It was equally as tempting to lie in one of those reading her book for the day. Hoa led them around the side of the now silent aviary to an outbuilding and opening the screen door she flicked the light on. 'This is the breakfast room, please help yourself in the morning,' she said smiling. There was a fridge humming and a small electric stove top for frying but most importantly there was a kettle with a jar of Nescafe next to it along with a container which presumably held teabags. All was good in her world, Moira thought, as she followed Hoa's lead, turning the light off on her way out.

They scurried behind the sweeping torch as she led them down the path toward the bungalows. 'You are in number three. Be careful there is a step.'

Voices called out hello in the darkness and as Hoa opened the door and the light flickered on they spied a couple sitting wrapped in a blanket on the adjacent veranda. They were stargazing as they sipped from their bottles of beer and Mammy, never one to miss an opportunity, introduced herself and Moira. The brief ensuing chat revealed them both to be Swedish.

'Mammy, you're letting all the bugs in standing out here, say goodnight,' Moira whispered, seeing Hoa waiting patiently inside for them.

Their bags were already miraculously in the room, leaning against the far wall of the cosy space, and Moira guessed the kindness would be down to Sang, Hoa and Binh's oldest child. She made a note to self to thank him in the morning. 'It's lovely, so it is. We'll be very comfortable in here won't we, Moira? Thank you, Hoa.'

'Yes, it's grand, thank you, Hoa.'

Their hostess looked pleased. 'I say goodnight now.' She beamed.

'Goodnight.' Moira and Maureen chimed.

Mammy and daughter did their ablutions and then turning the light out clambered in to the bed they were to share. It creaked under their bodyweight as they snuggled down under the blankets. They lay, eyes growing used to the darkness, talking over what a wonderful night it had been until Mammy yawned. 'I think I'll have to shut my eyes now, Moira. Keep to your side of the bed do you hear?'

'It's not me who thinks she's a starfish,' Moira replied before partaking of her nightly routine of plumping her pillow and twisting and turning until she was satisfied this was as good as it was going to get. She lay listening to the silence which was absolute apart from Mammy's snuffly breathing and the odd plop of a fish. She was, she realised, giving a contented little sigh, feeling very Zen. The world was a wondrous place. It was then she heard a high-pitched whine buzz past her ear. 'Oh for feck's sake,' she muttered hauling herself upright.

'I was nearly asleep then, Moira. What's the problem?'

'There's a mosquito buzzing about.' She got out of bed and padded the short distance across the wooden floors to the door where the light switch was. The room flooded with light and Maureen squinted into it none too pleased at the sudden brightness. She made a guttural grumping sound.

'What? I can't sleep with that thing buzzing around.' Moira's eyes flicked wildly around the space trying to locate the culprit.

'Sure there's nothing here it probably flew out through the bathroom window. Put the light out, I'm knackered so I am.'

'Mammy,' Moira's tone was indignant, 'have you forgotten the time you left Aisling and Rosi in charge and you, me and Daddy went to Rosslare for a weekend by the seaside? I got bitten on the eye and it swelled up something terrible. It was awful and I'm not long getting over the pink eye.'

Maureen hadn't forgotten. She could remember it clearly. Moira had been very dramatic about it all, as was her way, refusing to leave the bed and breakfast unless her parents provided her with a pair of Jacqui O sunglasses to hide behind. Thirteen was a trying age so it was, she and Brian had muttered, setting off to find a shop that sold oversized black sunglasses. Now she sighed heavily. There was something about that girl and her eyes when she was on her holidays. She also knew what her youngest daughter was like when she got a bee in her bonnet. If you can't beat em, best join em.

A flickering movement caught her eye and she clambered out of bed picking up her paperback. The sooner the thing was dealt with the sooner they could put the light out and get some sleep. *Aha, there it was.* Maureen crept stealthily over to the wall and thwacked her book against it. She missed and the spindly creature twirled teasingly, up out of her reach. She used bad language as did Moira after her ensuing near misses. The minutes passed with the pair of them leaping and thudding about the room. This was getting personal. Until Moira in a rage leapt up onto the bed clutching a flip-flop and swinging blindly.

'I think you got it.' Maureen cried; she was as invested in getting the beasty thing now as Moira. It was a matter of pride; she wouldn't be beaten by a four-legged, flying bug.

Moira stopped swinging and inspected the sole of the flip-flop, 'Yes!' She held it out showing Mammy the splayed mosquito embedded on its sole. 'Got the fecker, she said thudding down to the floor. 'Don't mess with Moira O'Mara.'

'The poor Swedes will wonder what's going on in here,' Maureen said, half expecting a knock on the door as she put the light out and climbed back into bed.

They slept like babies after that.

Chapter 27

Maureen and Moira found Sally-Ann once they'd showered and dressed the next morning. She was setting about making a pot of tea in the building Hoa had shown them the night before and seeing this Moira could have kissed her. She'd kill for a brew. Pouring the boiling water into the pot, Sally-Ann told them she'd spent the night in the house with the family, Binh, having assured her there was room, had been insistent she stay with them. 'He said I was part of the family,' she said smiling from mother to daughter. 'Thank you for coming here with me.'

'Not a bother. Sure it's a lovely part of the world from what we saw yesterday. And we were very comfortable in our bungalow last night weren't we, Moira.'

Moira put the grapefruit she'd been inspecting back in the bowl and agreed.

Their Swedish neighbours were just finishing clearing up their breakfast things. 'Good morning,' they greeted in their clipped, precise English. They had some serious looking hiking gear on and the admiration shining in Mammy's eyes made Moira smile to herself. She was developing a thing for outdoor, active wear. Morning pleasantries were exchanged before the tall, athletic looking couple headed off to tackle their action-packed plans for the day.

An assortment of fresh fruits; melon, papaya, bananas and grapefruit had been laid out for the guests to help themselves.

There was a loaf of bread for toasting and fresh eggs could be fried on the stove top if so desired. Moira settled for banana on toast and sat down to enjoy it at the little wooden table in the corner along with her cup of tea. Sally-Ann and Mammy busied themselves frying eggs. She could detect, in between bites and sips, the genuine happiness in the Australian woman's voice as she told Mammy she hadn't gone to bed until late because there'd been so much to talk about. She was overjoyed, she said at how welcome the family had made her feel. It was unexpected and it was a joy.

They sat down with Moira and ate their food to a background symphony of birds before washing up.

'Moira and I thought we might cycle into the village today. Would you like to join us, Sal? We think we'll stay tonight, if the bungalow isn't booked—I'll check with Hoa and Binh on our way out. And I know Binh said we were his guests but we'll be paying our way.'

Moira nodded her agreement.

'Moira wants to pick up some more mosquito repellent and I'm eager to have a look at the handicrafts on offer. We'll sort out a way of getting back to Hue when we're in the village too and, if it all goes to plan, make our way back there tomorrow for a night before getting the bus to Hanoi. Do you know what your plans are yet?' Maureen finally stopped to draw breath and Sally-Ann leaped into the opening.

'If you don't mind, I'd like to stay around here today and help Hoa, repay her for her hospitality and get a feel for this place. They farm organically and I'm curious to see how it all works. I haven't thought any further than that.' Sally-Ann shrugged.

'Fair play to you.' Mammy, who was on drying, said before wiping the last plate and popping it back into the dish rack.

'OOH I HAVEN'T BEEN on one of these in years,' Maureen shrieked, she'd had a bit of difficulty cocking her leg over the bar initially but now she was happily wobbling her way around the area where Danh had parked yesterday. She was doing a few practice circuits, ringing her bell a couple of times for good measure. She liked the bell. The big, hairy dog whose name was Wag was sitting in the shade of the banana trees watching her antics his tail thumping sporadically.

'Come on, Mammy, let's go. You'll be grand.' Moira was impatient to get moving. 'Just follow me and keep in to the left if you hear anything coming.' She pedalled toward the entrance.

Maureen drew alongside her. 'I should go in the lead, I think, Moira. What with me being older.'

'That's exactly why I should go in the front. Besides I know what I'm doing.'

Maureen gave a snort. 'You do not! Sure, you're all knees on that thing.'

'At least I can ride in a straight line, you're steering it like you're on your way home from a night on the lash.'

There was a stand-off as they eyed one another and if they'd had engines, they would have revved them. Their matching hazel eyes challenged one another until Moira broke away to pedal up the road as fast as she could, her dark hair streaming out behind her.

'That's not fair,' Maureen cried, frantically pumping her legs to catch up. 'Slow down, Moira, I can't keep up.'

Moira looked back over her shoulder. 'I'll go in the front on the way there and you can be in the lead on the way back, alright?' She knew a compromise was going to have to be reached because she wasn't fit enough to keep this pace up all the way to the village.

Maureen seemed to accept that, slowing to a more leisurely pace so she could enjoy the unfolding scenery.

Moira stopped pedalling and coasting along, she too looked around her. A light mist still clung to the rice paddies giving the fields a mystical, lost in time aura. The lone water buffalo she could see appeared as a ghostly spectre plodding along with birds hitching a ride on his knobbly back. A large black-winged hawk, or at least that's what she thought it was, soared starkly against the cloudless sky. The only sound was that of her own puffing breath as she tried to catch it. It was broken a few beats later by the familiar labouring sound of an approaching moped and she called back over her shoulder for Mammy to keep in.

'I know what I'm doing thank you, Moira,' Maureen shouted back veering dangerously close to the verge which dropped down into the waterway. She righted herself in the nick of time, pleased Moira hadn't witnessed her near miss and, as the children on the scooter passed by, the one on the back waving to her, she rang her bell.

They passed the vegetable plots Moira recalled seeing from the minivan yesterday which signalled they weren't far from the village. She saw the farmers with their heads shaded by their conical hats, baskets on their back as they went about their tasks. She also saw a bridge up ahead and a flash of red in the middle of it. She looked closer.

'Look over there.' Moira gestured to the stone bridge. It led away from the edge of the village and across to the rice paddies. A minivan pulled up and idled while a group of sightseers piled out. They formed an orderly line beside the stone walkway and Moira guessed they must be British. Nobody knew how to wait in a queue quite like the Brits. She cycled closer before braking to see what it was they were waiting for. An older woman, her silvered hair pulled back into a bun, was sitting on a mat in the middle of the bridge. She was wearing a red padded jacket and it was this that had initially caught Moira's eye as she rode along. A rangy young blonde woman, wearing pants not dissimilar to Moira's elephant ones but in blue, was crouched next to her and the old woman held her upturned palm in her hand; she was tracing a finger along it.

Mammy pulled up alongside Moira and they watched the interaction, along with the huddled group waiting their turn, curiously. The driver of the van came and stood alongside them. 'What's going on?' Maureen asked him.

'Her name is Mother Bui, she's the Love Fortune Teller of Mui Ha Bridge. Very popular with the tourists. She tell you what is going to happen with you in the future for a donation.' He grinned, no gold tooth on display but he did have an impressive hole where one of his front teeth should have been. 'You want your fortune told?' He grinned at Moira who was listening intently and gestured to the back of the line. Moira nodded eagerly; she liked the sound of this. She liked the sound of it a lot and getting off her bike, she kicked the stand down. Maureen did the same and they stood at the back of the short line.

It wasn't long before the blonde woman stood up and they watched while she unzipped her bum bag retrieving a wad of notes which she placed in the dish next to the old woman. The old woman rewarded her with a gummy smile and a nod and the blonde made her way back across the bridge. Her face was flushed pink and a smile was playing at the corners of her mouth.

Moira collared her as she walked past. 'What was it like?'

'Mother Bui? She was great. I mean wow—she, like, knew so much.' The girl looked to be around the same age as Moira with a Californian valley-girl inflection. 'She mentioned the guy who broke up with me recently straight off, and then she told me there's someone else waiting to meet me but first I need to get to know what's in here.' She tapped her white singlet-clad chest and Moira thought she really should have put a bra on, what with the slight chill the sun had yet to ward off. 'And you know, like, that's why I'm here. I realised I, like, had no sense of who I was after my ex and I split. I'd spent so long trying to be the kind of girl I thought he wanted that I, like, didn't know who I was anymore.'

Moira smiled and shifted a little uncomfortably, too much, like, information. 'Well, I'm glad things are going to work out for you.'

The girl smiled, she was very pretty in that wholesome no make-up, beachy kind of way. She reached out and rested her hand fleetingly on Moira's forearm. 'I hope you, like, hear whatever it is you want to hear, too.' And she went on her way.

Mammy who'd been listening dropped in, 'They're very forthcoming, the Americans. They like to share.'

Moira thought this amusing given Mammy would tell a lamp post her life story if there was no one else about. 'Are you going to have your palm read?' she asked.

'I am.' Maureen's nod was emphatic. 'Sure, I want to know what's on the road ahead of me as much as the next girl.'

Moira side-eyed her mammy. It was disconcerting to think of the possibility of her with anyone other than Daddy. On the other side of the coin it was sad to think of her on her own for the rest of her days. Come to that, neither option was something she liked to think about. Mammy wasn't over the hill just yet though, this holiday had reinforced that. Sure look it, she'd had a beer-bellied German give her the glad eye and taken to her bicycle like a duck to water. She was beginning to understand that Mammy wasn't just her mammy, she was a woman in her own right. It was quite a startling thought. Referring to herself as a girl was a bit of a stretch though.

She wished the middle-aged man with the combover flapping in the gentle breeze would get a move on—surely his romantic future couldn't be that involved. A thought occurred to her. 'Mammy you're not to be earwigging on what she has to say to me.' If she were to overhear whatever this Mother Bui revealed it would hit the O'Mara women's telegraph faster than a speeding bullet. Her sisters would read far more into what was divulged than was healthy, especially Rosi with her being into all that new agey stuff, she'd take it as gospel. No, Moira decided, she'd listen but she'd take whatever she was told lay ahead for her in the love department with a pinch of salt. Especially if she didn't like what Mother Bui had to say.

Maureen shot her a withering glance, 'Back at yer. I don't want you listening in on what she tells me either, thank you very much.' She knew if Moira's big ears were flapping then whatever this Mother Bui had to say would be communicated to her daughters faster than the speed of light *and* they'd all read far too much into whatever it was she was told. No, she resolved, she'd be sensible and take whatever she heard on this bridge in the next while with a grain of salt. Unless of course she was told yer man, Daniel Day Lewis, was going to be making an appearance in the near future.

The line eventually shortened as the last of the happy customers clambered back into the van, assured of their romantic destiny and ready to head to their next port of call. Moira looked at her mammy. 'You can go first.'

'No, after you.'

A brief skirmish in the reverse order of their earlier discussion over the bikes ensued before Moira, receiving a push in her back from Mammy, set off toward Mother Bui. She checked over her shoulder to make sure Mammy wasn't following her. The old woman had watched their exchange with amusement, and her face was lit up in welcome as she gestured for Moira to sit down in front of her. She knelt down and as she looked into Mother Bui's eyes, she found herself thinking of raisins; they were crinkled, dark, and sweet, but more than that they held the kind of wisdom gleaned from a long life led.

She held out her hand seeking Moira's who placed hers trustingly in Mother Bui's. The fortune teller stared at her palm for a long time and Moira was beginning to get antsy, *this couldn't be good.*

'Your heart it has been broken.' She tapped her chest with her spare hand. 'Not long, yes?'

Moira nodded, her English was very good, she got brownie points for that, but she wasn't handing any out for her summation just yet, even if it was on the mark. It was, after all an easy guess. Sure, half the people who walked across this bridge to see her were bound to have had their hearts broken at some point. It was the stuff of life.

'He married.'

Moira shifted uncomfortably now; this she couldn't shrug off.

Mother Bui traced a finger down one of the lines on her palm and shook her head, a silvered wisp escaping and floating around her face. 'He no good for you.'

Moira found herself nodding her agreement, she was holding her breath.

'I see a man. He much better, you will have much happiness together.'

Moira sat back on her haunches breathing out in a long, slow hiss. *Did she have his phone number?* Her nerves had abated now she knew she wasn't destined for spinsterhood and she smiled at Mother Bui unsure whether she'd finished her reading.

'He a healer. A man of medicine. A good man.'

Moira thought of Tom, *please let her mean Tom,* her insides grew warm and fluid as she conjured up his surfer boy good looks. They'd have beautiful babies, so they would.

'He have very nice,' Mother Bui patted her rump and she grinned her gummy grin. Moira looked at her in surprise and then her face split into a wide grin.

'He does.'

A few minutes later, and five American dollars poorer, she made her way back across the uneven cobbles of the bridge to where she could see Mammy waiting chomping at the bit for her turn. She was a prophet that Mother Bui, Moira thought, unable to wipe her smile from her face.

'It obviously went well,' Mammy said seeing Moira's inane grin.

'She knew things, Mammy. She's the real deal.'

Maureen looked at her daughter for a second; she'd dearly love to know what she'd been told. Now would be the moment to squeeze it out of her too, while she was all starry-eyed and full of it. Two women around her age in the unmistakable clobber of tourists came into her line of vision. They were making their way from the village toward the bridge. She'd not have them pushing in, she decided, and with that she lolloped over the bridge toward Mother Bui, eager to hear what she would say.

Chapter 28

Maureen walked back to where Moira was waiting for her. She still had a sappy look on her face. She, however, was feeling rather odd. She hadn't known what she wanted to hear, not really. She supposed she'd wanted to know that she'd be alright. That one day the awful aching void inside her, that no amount of filling every waking moment helped ease, would abate. If it did though, would that mean she was letting go of Brian? It was the fear of losing the part of him she carried with her that made her cling to that ache. Mother Bui had seemed to know all this. She'd certainly known her heart hurt and she'd told her that the pain would stop and it wouldn't mean she'd stopped loving her husband. She said she had a very big heart and could love more than once. She'd also told her to watch for a man with grey eyes and hair. She'd tapped her own hair and then she'd made a swimming motion with her hand as she said he was a man of the water. It was this man who would bring back her smile but only if she let him.

Obviously, Maureen thought, ignoring Moira's questioning gaze as she asked what took her so long, that meant he enjoyed sailing. She was pleased she'd had the red dress made for the Christmas party just in case this man with grey eyes and hair happened to be there. She wasn't ready for any sort of a thing with anyone. She didn't know if she ever would be. But sure, that didn't mean she couldn't look her best, now did it? She kicked the stand up on her bike.

Both women were quiet as they cycled the short distance to the main street they'd passed through the day before. They parked their bikes on a spare bit of pavement, confident nobody would try and pinch them, as they set off to have a look around. There were wooden artefacts on display everywhere and piled up pots, varnished to a high gloss spilled out onto the pavement they were wandering down. If a pot wasn't up your alley then there was furniture for sale of a similar style to that which they'd admired inside Binh and Hoa's home. Maureen ran her hand over an occasional table. That would look lovely in her living room. She refused to call it a sitting room. Her apartment was far too modern to have a sitting room. She looked at it longingly but knew she'd never get it home. An intricately carved wall hanging caught her attention. 'Whoever's after making this is very clever. Look at the detail in it, Moira.'

'Mm,' she replied. It was very busy, lovely if you liked grinning gargoyles and lots of them. 'What's going on over there?' She pointed to a shop across the road with an open frontage. Three men were cross-legged on woven mats surrounded by wood shavings as they chipped away at lumps of wood. A handful of curious observers stood around them watching or snapping photos as they worked.

'Come on, we'll go and see for ourselves.'

'Mammy, look where you're going!' Moira yelped, pulling her mother back from the path of an oncoming scooter.

'I saw it, Moira, thank you.'

Moira shook her head knowing full well she hadn't, she had tunnel vision at times, like a toddler with their destination in sight, oblivious to what was going on around them. So, mumbling words beginning with f and liability under her breath she trailed behind her.

They joined the huddle and watched as hunks of wood were shaped into religious deities, elephants, and dragons. They were artists these men and it was fascinating to observe their deft actions as they chipped something from nothing. One of the men picked up a chunk of wood, a piece that would nicely feed a fire, and held out his chisel gesturing for one of the onlookers to have a turn. Maureen just about fell over herself in her eagerness to push the gentleman, clad in travel pants just like hers only with fewer pockets, out the way.

Tunnel vision, Moira thought to herself once more, trying not to laugh as Mammy took hold of the chisel. She knelt there on the mat for a moment observing how the other two carpenters were holding theirs. Then, tongue poking out the corner of her mouth in concentration, she began to gouge lumps out of her wood.

The minutes ticked by and a few of the group dropped away. They'd clearly decided they didn't want to stand here until teatime when the woman with the beaded braids finally finished whatever it was she was trying to do. 'C'mon, Mammy, you've been ages and it still doesn't look like anything.' Moira shifted from foot to foot; she too was growing impatient. We all have talents in life, she thought to herself, and woodwork was not one of Mammy's.

'Don't rush me, Moira.' She brandished the chisel at her, brow furrowed, before getting back to work. Finally, she sat back on her heels and proclaimed she was finished.

Moira half expected a cheer to go up.

'Very good. Very good.' The man whose chisel it was snatched it back before she could change her mind.

There was a polite round of applause from those that had hung in there for the duration as Maureen held her creation aloft for them to admire. It looked to the untrained eye like a banana and Moira asked for confirmation of this as she hauled Mammy from the shop. 'Is it one of those wooden fruits you display in a bowl?' It would look rather on odd all on its lonesome but she didn't fancy Mammy's chances of being allowed to sit down again in order to chip out an orange or an apple.

'No, it is not. It's a canoe.' Maureen's tone suggested this should have been obvious. She would've liked to have tried her hand at a junk but she didn't think she'd be able to manage the complicated sails so she'd settled on a more straightforward but still seaworthy vessel.

'Jaysus, Mammy, it's just come to me what it reminds me of.' Moira almost snorted her tonsils up through her nostrils.

'If you're going to be rude—'

'A man's bits. I'm telling you right now, Mammy, you're not bringing that home with us. Sure, if you get stopped at customs, they'll think you're after trying to import some sort of fertility effigy.' She eyed the offensive looking lump of wood in her mammy's hand and began giggling.

Maureen huffed. 'You've a dirty mind, so you do. I'm sure I don't know what company you've been keeping but it's not like any man's privates I've ever seen.'

Postcards

DEAR PATRICK,

It's your mammy here. Moira and I are in the village of Mui Ha which is a few hour's drive from Hue where we got off our hop on, hop off bus. I'll telephone you to tell you the story of how we came to be here when we get home. It's like something from a film so be sure to make time in your schedule to talk to me. We're staying on a farm with a main house and bungalow accommodation for the guests, it's gorgeous. We've been made to feel like family by the owners. Our bungalow has a veranda which overlooks a pond, and there's a hammock which Moira's spent a lot of time today swinging on. She likes listening to the fish plopping about. I haven't had a look-in but sure that's no bad thing. I don't think I'd be able to get back out of it. Yesterday we explored the village. The wood carvings which are a local specialty are beautiful and good value but sadly mostly too big to bring home. I had a go at the carving and made you something. I'll give it to you when we see you next.

Love Mammy

MAUREEN COULDN'T BRING herself to ask after his big-breasted girlfriend, besides she'd run out of room, her writing had grown so tiny as she'd tried to squeeze all she wanted to say in that it was barely decipherable. She put the card aside and set about penning the next one.

DEAR ROSEMARY,

It's Maureen here. Moira and I are having a grand time. We're two and a half hours from Hue in a village called Mui Ha. We're staying in a very nice bungalow on a farm-stay which is down to my new Australian friend, Sally-Ann, and we're being treated like royalty. I can't wait to tell you how we came to be here but it's a long story and it will have to wait until we get home. It's very beautiful here. Very peaceful. The sun is beginning to set and I am sitting on the veranda of our bungalow. Moira is swinging back and forth on the hammock; she won't let me get a look-in. There's a pond in front of me and it's like glass apart from ripples now and again from the fish swimming about in it. I can see the mountains behind us reflected in the water. It's a mirror image and everything around us is bathed in a golden light, even Moira. She looks like yer woman from Goldfinger. I hope the weather is not too grim at home.

Yours, Maureen

HA! EAT YOUR HEART out, Rosemary. She hoped it was raining cats and dogs in Howth today. It would serve her right for cancelling on her the way she had. Still and all, if she hadn't then Moira and her, wouldn't be here together and that was something she wouldn't swap for all the tea in China. She looked at her daughter fondly for a moment before setting to writing her last card.

DEAR NOAH,

It's your nana here. Aunty Moira and I are having a grand time. We're staying in the village of Mui Ha on a farm-stay where there are chickens and fish, real ones not crumbed like the fish fingers and chicken burgers you're always asking your mammy for. It's not a farm like how we think of one though, more a place to stay in the country. They grow grapefruit, vegetables and rice here. The village is well known for its woodwork and we watched the carpenters turning pieces of wood into all manner of things. I got to have a turn and I made a canoe. Aunty Moira has been very rude about it but I'm very pleased with it. We were only going to stay for one night but we liked it so much we stayed for three. I hope you are being a good boy for your mammy and dad - give then a hug from me and have one for yourself.

Love Nana

Chapter 29

Mammy's Travel Journal

Hello from Hanoi. We've been here two days and are now fully recovered from the journey here. We travelled through the night from Hue and didn't get a wink between us. The bus was bursting at the seams and we were jammed in like sardines. On the bright side the roads were a lot better so we weren't in fear for our lives. It was our last leg on our hop on, hop off tickets. We're on our own from here on.

It was hard saying goodbye to Sal but it was time for us to move on from Mui Ha. We'd stayed an extra day as it was because it was so relaxing. I thought Moira's bottom had been welded to that hammock. Sal has decided to stay with Binh and Hoa for a while. There is plenty she can do to help earn her board and I think she feels she's found another home with them. I told her she has a home with us too whenever she wants to come and visit the Emerald Isle. She promised me she would come and see us one day soon. She's a golfer so we'd have a grand time on the Howth fairway so long as she decides to come in the summertime.

We didn't know what to buy the family to say thank you for their hospitality and saying thank you alone when they'd made us so very welcome wasn't enough. I thought about giving them my canoe but I'd already promised it to Patrick in the postcard I'd sent him and besides I don't think Moira would have let me. In the end we took the whole family for dinner at the restaurant in *the village and we had a lovely time. There was lots of laughter around our table and the food was very good. I especially enjoyed the rice dumplings Hoa suggested for dessert. It's a funny thing saying goodbye to people you feel so warm towards. It's not easy either to leave somewhere you've felt so, peaceful, is the only word I can think of to describe it. Moira and I were both reluctant to leave for Hue but we'd arranged a driver.*

His name was Phuc—I had to have words with Moira when we had a toilet stop because she kept repeating his name. It was all Phuc this and Phuc that. I told her she wasn't being clever if that's what she thought. She was exactly the same the time we had a guest stay with the surname Condon. I told her off back then too. Anyway I think Phuc might have got a bit tired of her talking in the end because he put his radio on loud and my ears were ringing by the time we got to Hue.

The sun had been up a couple of hours by the time the bus dropped us at a hotel in Hanoi's Old Quarter. It was the first one on our trip that was not up to standard. I didn't need to run my finger along the skirting to see that. It was a disgrace so it was and whoever their Director of Housekeeping is, she should be ashamed of herself. We said we wouldn't be staying to the girl on the desk who was too busy eating her pot noodles to care and as we stepped outside the touts were like a school of fish swarming us. It put me in mind of famous people when they're being mobbed by the paparazzi. It was not a nice experience especially because we were dead on our feet.

In the end we followed a man who assured us his hotel, was very clean and only a short walk away. It took ten minutes to get there, he took my bag for me which annoyed Moira no end. She moaned all the way there. I told her what doesn't kill you will make you stronger and that it was her own fault for packing her bag with enough gear in it to immigrate to Australia. She needs to wash her elephant pants too, I noticed, she's sat on something on the bus and I didn't have the heart to tell her she looked like she'd had an accident.

The Red River Hotel was an improvement on the last place but after checking out the shower I told Moira to be sure to wear her flip-flops in there because she didn't want to be going home with verrucas. Moira thought we should try and stay awake but I told her I was a woman of sixty who'd just survived an overnight bus trip, I needed an hour's sleep before venturing out again at least. Well, let me tell you, she was snoring before me. We'd set the alarm so as not to sleep the day away and got up at lunchtime.

There was plenty going on in the Old Quarter. It was hectic but not as busy as Hoi Chi Minh. Still and all we decided to visit Hoàn Kiếm Lake to escape the crowds. It wasn't far away and it was very pretty. Moira and I took turns having our photographs taken on the red bridge which leads to Jade Island in the middle of the lake. There's a pagoda there with lots of incense burning. The smell was a bit much for me but Moira said, sure it was no worse than me with the Arpège at Dublin airport. She's very taken with all the Buddhist temples and shrines we've seen. I'm beginning to wonder if the elephant pants were a good idea after all.

We slept for twelve hours solid that night and packed in a full day sightseeing given how bright eyed and bushy tailed we were the next morning. We visited the French Quarter which was very French and yer man Hoi Chi Minh's museum, partly because you can always find a toilet in a museum and partly because we thought we should. We also saw the Presidential Palace. Tonight we went to a water puppet show at a very beautiful theatre. I *wasn't sure if I was going to like it as Punch n Judy always frightened me but it was a gas. I loved every minute of it and I gave those puppeteers a standing ovation. Moira's after buying a puppet to bring home with her—at least it wasn't another lantern. I said she could supplement her income by doing a puppet show on Grafton Street.*

We've booked a day trip tomorrow to Ninh Binh which we were told is like Ha Long Bay but on land. The trip's very good value too with lunch included.

Postcards

DEAR TESSA

I said I'd send you a postcard so here it is. The picture on the front is of the view from Bich Dong, a pagoda built into a cave over three levels where Buddhist monks once lived. We climbed up there today before going on a sampan boat ride through the waterways which was very relaxing after all those stairs. I have thigh burn now. This trip with Mammy is not turning out how I thought it would. I thought we'd drive each other mad but we haven't. Well not much anyway. Mostly we've had a good craic and I never thought I'd say this but there's no one else I would have wanted to come away with. Not that I could have come with anyone else because I didn't have the airfare. Still and all, I feel like I've got to know another side of her since we've been here. We've seen and done some incredible things together including today's trip. I hope you're enjoying being back home. Has your

man, Owen, made any noises about visiting you? I'd like to come to New Zealand one day soon. This trip has made me want more.
    Your friend, Moira.

DEAR NOAH
    It's your nana here. Aunty Moira and I are in Hanoi which is the second biggest city in Vietnam. We've had a good look around and have decided we like it. It's an interesting city. You don't actually have to do anything. You can just find somewhere to sit and watch everything going on around you, because there's so much happening. We went to see a puppet show last night which was performed on water, can you believe that? We also explored a big cave three storeys high and I thought my knees might give out before we got to the top but they didn't. That was in a place called Ninh Binh where the landscape was like going back to the dinosaur era. Tomorrow we go to Ha Long Bay and I get to sail on a junk. I feel like you feel on the night before Christmas. I hope you're being a good boy for your mammy and dad give them a hug from me and have one for yourself.
    Love Nana

Chapter 30

'I can't walk down that. Sure, it's like walking the plank. Where are the hand rails?'

'Give the man your pack, Mammy, and then walk towards him. Sure you'll be grand.'

Maureen swung her pack at the crew member waiting for her at the other end of the gangway. He caught it, staggering back before placing it on the deck and holding his hand out to indicate Maureen should walk toward him. There was still a good few yards between where she was and he was. No man's land and this was what had her in a state. 'I'll wind up in the water for sure.'

'No you won't. It's only a few little steps, you can do it.'

'I can't.'

Moira's softly, softly approach wore thin. 'Listen to me, Mammy, you have to. How else are you going to get on the boat? They can't airlift you in.'

'Junk, Moira, it's called a junk. Look at the sails.' She pointed at the red concertina sails. 'I didn't come all this way just to go on a boat, now did I? Sure, I can do that at home whenever I like.' Her voice went up an octave as she eyed the wooden plank dangling over the water as it stretched from the wooden vessel in front of her to the wharf on which she was standing.

'Shall I go first? Would that make it easier?'

'No, I'm not after having you standing there looking at me like the cat that got the cream. I'll do it. Just give me a minute.' She shook her wrists like she was limbering up.

Moira heard an impatient cough. 'There's a queue behind us Mammy c'mon you can't be holding everybody up.'

Maureen's head did an exorcist style swivel and she only just missed slapping herself in the face with her beads as she turned to glare at the line behind her. 'Well,' she turned her attention back to Moira and said in a voice designed to carry, 'they can fecking well wait.' Fear was making her maniacal and Moira turned around and mouthed 'sorry' to her fellow passengers. They were being very understanding she thought, given the circumstances.

Maureen looked upward before crossing herself and following it up with a quick word with HIM upstairs before looking at Moira one last time. 'If I don't make it, I want you to know—'

'Jaysus, Mammy just get on the boa-junk, would ya!'

The very air itself seemed to hold its breath as she took a tentative first step onto the plank. She wavered for a moment before holding her hands out either side, then placed one foot daintily in front of the other like Roisin used to do on the balance bar at gymnastics when she was a child. One step, two steps, three steps. Her hand reached out and was clasped by a strong male grip as the crew member helped her down onto the deck.

A round of applause went up and Maureen preened before shouting across to them, 'It's alright once you're on it, just don't think about it too much and don't stop.'

Moira tossed her pack over and eyed the plank. 'Mammy, stop shouting you'll distract me.'

'C'mon, Moira, if I can do it, you can. On the count of three now.'

'Mammy, shut up!' Moira was terrified, not that she'd admit it, but there was a nasty drop either side of the plank into the oily swirling water below. What happened to health and safety? That's what she wanted to know. She heard that same cough again and, knowing she couldn't stand here all day she did what Mammy had said, counted to three and across she went.

She too got a smattering of applause but she refrained from shouting any helpful hints over to the beanpole in a light rain-jacket who she was fairly certain was the cougher. Instead she said, 'Let's go up there.' She pointed to the upstairs deck, 'and find somewhere to sit.' They passed through the main cabin filled with empty seats, and their bags, Moira saw, were already being stacked in an alcove. The stairs leading to the upstairs deck were at the rear and they made their way up them to a covered open-air seating area. They slid along a bench seat and took a moment to soak in their surroundings.

'Is it what you thought it would be like?' Moira asked.

Maureen sighed happily. 'It's better, the only thing missing is Roger.'

Moira thought of Roger the Rat; she was sure there were plenty in the hull below. It took her a moment or two to twig Mammy was referring to her favourite Bond actor. They both scowled, watching people lithely skip over the plank and leap onto the boat. It was unnatural, Moira thought, as Maureen stood up. 'Take my picture, Moira, with the sails in the background would you, before that bunch of prancers comes up here.'

Moira obliged, snapping away as Maureen struck different Bond girl poses until the first of the other passengers appeared at the top of the stairs. They sat back down as the seats around them began slowly filling, not wanting to lose their spot. The scene around them was a hub of activity as boats, cruise ships, and junks of varying sizes and shapes vied for space against the industrious wharf area. It was just as chaotic on the water as it had been on the roads in Hanoi, Maureen mused. She watched a crew member on the boat next door nimbly navigating his way from one end of the timber deck to the other. Down the way she could see fishermen checking over their nets. A thought popped into Maureen's head. 'Moira you don't get seasick, do you?'

'No, well at least I don't think so. The last boat I went on was the ferry in New York and I was grand on that.'

A couple were sitting in front of them and the man turned around; he was wearing a cap back to front and looked to be in his early twenties. 'I've got something if you're worried you might get sick.' His accent was peculiar, Moira thought, frowning as she tried to place it. *Australian maybe*? 'We're from South Africa,' he said reading her mind as he opened his satchel and while he was looking inside it his girlfriend glanced back.

'You don't want to be sick and miss the cruise,' she smiled. 'The scenery is going to be fabulous.' Her partner produced a glass vial. 'Just take one, it might help.'

Moira took the bottle thinking she'd be doing him a favour because if she was sick it was his back that would wear it. 'Thanks.'

'Oh no, you don't.' Maureen snatched the glass bottle from her daughter's hand and holding it out tried to read the label before giving up and retrieving her reading glasses.

'What are you doing?' Moira asked out the corner of her mouth, giving an apologetic smile to the South African man.

'Listen Moira it could be anything in here.' She shook the bottle. 'Bangkok Hilton *remember*?' This was said as though it were code between them and Moira had had enough, she took the bottle back.

'Yer man here is not after asking me to take it home through customs he's offering me a tablet to help settle my stomach for fecks sake.' She rolled her eyes at the man who was now looking from mother to daughter as though they'd just come down from Mars.

Mammy remained unrepentant. Moira helped herself to a tablet and swallowed it dry. 'Thanks for that, and sorry about—' she tilted her head toward her mammy. 'She watched a film before we left. You might have seen it. Nicole Kidman gets set up as she leaves Bangkok by a fella who comes across as being all nice and that and she winds up in prison. My mammy's very impressionable.'

He nodded as though he totally understood before elbowing his girlfriend. 'We might go and sit downstairs, I think. It's a bit cold up here.' And off they went.

'See what you did? He thinks we're mad.'

'Well if you start seeing enormous spiders climbing up the walls don't come crying to me.'

The boat juddered as the engine grumbled from deep within its bowel. Maureen clutched Moira's arm. 'We're off!'

At first all the two women could see ahead of them were mist shrouded monoliths rearing up from the dark, mysterious water. Behind them the skyline of high-rise hotels was growing smaller and the cruise ships that had looked so enormous while they were berthed had taken on a Lilliput-like quality. As they bobbed gently over the calm body of water it was as though they were looking through a camera lens and the subject was slowly coming into focus. The oily seawaters lapping the wharf were forgotten as the mists dispersed and they found themselves surrounded by an emerald sea. It was like a bolt of rippling silk, Moira thought, pleased with the analogy. The limestone pillars with their carpet of green came into sight and she overheard an English couple seated behind them talking. There were one thousand six hundred islands in the bay, and they were entering the first cluster of them.

Houseboats with waving families dotted the area and Moira found herself staring upwards in wonder at a Buddhist pagoda on top of a sheer, soaring column of rock. It defied belief as to how it had been built. She got up and moved to the railings, snapping away with her camera. Maureen came and stood alongside her. 'Mammy, I think this is the most beautiful sight I've ever seen.' Maureen linked her arm through her daughter's.

'Me too, Moira. I won't forget this for the rest of my days.'

Chapter 31

Mammy's Travel Journal

Hello from Cat Ba Island in Ha Long Bay where Moira and I are spending the night. Tonight I am a happy woman. I sailed on a junk today and it was everything and more I thought it would be. I felt like I'd stepped back in time. The journey through the island groups of limestone rocks and the emerald waters here to Cat Ba was breathtaking. We saw houseboats bobbing about, home to several generations. I got a bit uptight when Moira wouldn't stop harping on about your Buddhist temple plonked on top of a big rock. I was pleased when we moored up so we could explore a cave called 'Amazing Cave'. It got her off the topic. Walking into the cave was like having landed on the moon, it was a lunar landscape. We'd entered another world with razor sharp stalactites dripping from the roof, we walked deeper and deeper into it and saw caverns that looked like fairy grottos. The cave must have been underwater at some point because we could see the wave patterns worn into the ceiling.

We watched the sunset from our junk, a magical experience, before mooring at Cat Ba. Even though the light was dusky we could see as we trudged to our hotel that it isn't an island paradise. There's construction going on everywhere and road works. It's a work in progress and I think if we were to come back in a few years we wouldn't recognise the place. We enjoyed our dinner which was *included in the price of our hotel for the night. It was very good value. We get breakfast too.*

Afterward to work off our meal Moira and I went for a stroll down to the water. The moon was out and it was lighting a path across the black waters. The shadowy outlines of the junks that had brought us and all the other tourists to the island were moored for the night, waiting to take us back to the mainland in the morning. Above us millions of stars danced and we sat on a rock and just let it all wash over us.

I felt very grateful to HIM upstairs and I told him so. Something else too, I felt hopeful. This was new. I've not felt hopeful in a good while. The thing is I knew sitting there on that rock with Moira skimming pebbles that whatever happens next, I'm going to be grand. What's ahead of me is not what I thought it would be but I have to accept that because I can't change things. I don't think I understood that before we came here to Vietnam, not properly anyway. I realised I've so much to be grateful for in my life and at that moment as I saw a shooting star streak across the sky, I felt overwhelmed by gratitude.

Oh and I've decided I'm going to get a dog too. Not a big one, a little one I can sit on my lap. It's not healthy sitting alone and imagining Brian's still with me. I've not been helping myself and sure, he'd have been the first to tell me if I'm not careful I'll send myself doolally. I think he'd approve of a dog. We can go for walks along the pier together. It will be good company so it will.

Tomorrow we're getting the bus to Sa Pa. It's our last destination before heading back to Hanoi to fly home. This holiday's after going awfully quick all of a sudden. Moira and I have been reading in the guide book and we decided that we will do an independent trek. I'm looking forward to it and told Moira she's to take lots of photos because I will be giving a talk on our Vietnamese rambling experience for my fellow Howth ramblers when we get home.

Postcard

DEAR NOAH,

It's your nana here. Aunty Moira and I are on an island called Cat Ba in Ha Long Bay. We sailed here today on a junk which is a ship with big red sails like a fan. It was a dream come true for me. I hope when you're grown up your dreams come true too Noah. There were mountains rearing up out of the water which was a very unusual shade of green. We saw families living on houseboats. Big, extended families, the mammy, the daddy, the children and the grandparents on both sides sometimes too. Imagine living with me, your mammy, daddy, and your granny and gramps! Sure, one of us would get pushed off the boat. We also explored an enormous cave which had very sharp stalactites (ask mammy what they are). It looked like somewhere magic that fairies might live. I hope you're being a good boy for your mammy and dad give them a hug from me and have one for yourself.

Love Nana

Chapter 32

Moira breathed a sigh of relief as the bus pulled up outside Sa Pa's main post office. The last leg of their journey here as the bus wound its way higher and higher into the mountains until, looking at the swirling mists, she'd thought they were in the clouds, had seemed interminable. Her stomach had behaved itself thanks to Sally-Ann having insisted Mammy take what was left of the ginger sweets but she'd still felt it roll ominously around every hairpin bend. They pulled their day packs down from the overhead luggage holder and shrugged into jackets before following the rest of their weary travellers as they exited the bus. Their backpacks were already unloaded by the time they set their feet down on the pavement, and they helped one another on with them. 'We don't have to go far do we, Mammy?' Moira asked, stooped over as she eyed their fellow passengers marching down the street.

'God Almighty, Moira, you wouldn't last five minutes with one of them milkmaid's yokes.' The beads clacked as she shook her head.

It was cool enough here for a hat, Moira thought, sniffing the air. It'd be a relief if Mammy wore one and she didn't have to look at those braids. They hadn't grown on her. There was a definite alpine bite to the air, a sharp contrast to what it had been like when they began their trip in the south and she'd felt like she'd be smothered by the heady humidity. Come to think of it, she thought, jiggling the pack, one of those carrying poles would probably be a better option. It felt like the weight was all on one side of her pack and she was sure by the time she took it off she'd be like Quasimodo. She followed in Mammy's wake looking around her as she went.

'The book says the main centre is only down there, Moira, and that the place is overrun with hotels, we'll decide what we like the sound of when we get there.'

This wasn't the quaint little town in the hills she'd envisaged, Moira thought. The place was heaving with tourists from all destinations and the touts were out in force. Here and there through the teeming chaos she caught a glimpse of a colourful local. The buildings, while not high rises by any means, still closed in on the street they were on and she was sure when darkness descended the place would be awash with flickering neon lights. They came to a square and if they'd had any doubt they were in the right town it was assuaged by the wooden monument in the middle of it. The bottom circular tiers were filled with greenery and on the triangular centrepiece the words Sa Pa had been laid out in a vivid yellow flower of some sort.

Maureen leafed through the guide book while Moira looked about. It was a strange sorta place. Not one thing or the other. From what she could see, some of the buildings in the distance spreading down the hillside were like those you'd find in a French Alps ski resort while her closer surrounds were a maze-like concrete jungle, a miniature version of Hoi Chi Minh or Hanoi. It felt, she thought, as though it had spread rapidly to accommodate all its visitors but with no town planning or thought to how it would look when it all came together.

Maureen read her expression. 'It's a base, Moira, people come to visit the villages nearby and to trek. We're going to have a grand time here, so we are.'

A light rain began to fall and Moira eyed her mammy. The last time she'd used that cajoling 'It's going to be jolly good fun' tone on her was when they'd set off on their epic O'Mara family road trip around the Ring of Kerry. It hadn't reassured her then and it wasn't reassuring her now.

'I've my eye on a hotel, it sounds like it's very good value. C'mon it should be down that road over there. Let's get out of this rain.'

Postcard

DEAR NOAH,

The picture on the front is of Ta Phin Village in Sa Pa where the Red Dao people live, they're famous for their red dao leaf bath salts. The village is full of massage spas with bathtubs full of the stuff. They're sorta like the bubbles your mammy puts in your bath only these ones make the water red and the smell off them or whatever else goes in with it is gorgeous. Nana and I sat in a tub together and even though it was weird to sit in a bath with her it was also very relaxing because we were looking out over the rice terraces. I think Nana was responsible for the bubbles in our bath too. She said she felt like a girl of twenty again when she got out. I don't think she'll be saying that when we get back from our trek tomorrow. I have run out of room so I am going to write another card.

Love Aunty Moira.

DEAR NOAH,

The picture on the front is of the rice terraces here around Sa Pa. The villagers in Ta Phin wear bright colourful layers of clothes and are very smiley even though they don't have television. Imagine that Noah? No Thomas the Tank or Postman Pat. There were lots of handicrafty things for sale too. I had to stop Nana from buying a coat in the local brocade. It's a handmade fabric the people here wear like on the other card I'm sending you which looks grand on them. She did buy lots of cushion covers though and a hat which she is going to wear on our trek tomorrow. I don't know why she went on at me about my lanterns because her living room is going to look like an ethnic minority village by the time she's finished. It's quite cold here and I didn't like Sa Pa much when we first arrived. It wasn't what I expected but having seen more today, I've changed my mind. Be good for your mam.

Love Aunty Moira.

Chapter 33

'Mammy I don't know if I'm able for this.' Moira's head spun as she leaned over to tie the laces of the walking boots she'd lugged the length of the country.

Maureen pulled the little black hat with the band of brocade around the bottom down low over her ears and inspected herself in the mirror. She was pleased with her purchase; she looked the part so she did. She had thermal leggings on underneath her quick dry pants and a special thermal insulating top she'd invested in under her rain jacket. She looked at Moira's reflection, she was sitting on the bed with a face on her that could curdle milk. 'Sure, we've come all this, we're not going home without rambling. I trained for months for this, Moira, you know that.'

Traipsing around the hills and calling in at the local pubs for a refresher along the way with a few old faithfuls like Rosemary Farrell and the rest of the Howth Ramblers wasn't what Moira would call training. 'But I've not had a wink of sleep.' She really hadn't. There'd been a non-stop row of door slamming and loud drunk sounding indecipherable voices echoing throughout the hotel for the best part of the night. At four am, fed up, Moira got up and stuck her head out the door, set to have a go at whoever was behind the current ruckus. There'd been no one there and she realised it wasn't even coming from their floor. The sound was carrying from somewhere below. She'd wished nasty things on the arse responsible along with the builders for not soundproofing the place before slamming their door shut.

'Neither have I but once we get out there amongst the rice terraces in that lovely fresh air, we'll forget all about it. You've a good breakfast in you to see you through. C'mon, Moira, you'll be grand. And I've got scroggin.' She held up the bag of seeds and nuts she'd put together at the market yesterday.

'Oh, feck off with your scroggin, Mammy,' Moira said standing up. Chocolate might have seen her muster some enthusiasm but scroggin was obviously as good as it was going to get.

Her boots, never worn, were stiff on her feet and she hoped she wouldn't get blisters. Mammy had assured her the trek she'd picked for them to do would be a picnic, but sure, who'd trust a woman who looked like that, Moira thought, shooting the hat a look of disgust. It looked grand on the local people, but it looked ridiculous on the short Irish woman presently warming up in her active wear. 'C'mon then, let's get this over and done with.'

'That's not a very sporting attitude, Moira,' Maureen chided as she locked the door behind them.

Moira eyeballed every guest they passed as they made their way down to the reception area just in case they were one of the noisy arses from the night before.

'Right,' Mammy flapped the fold-out map she'd picked up from the reception clerk yesterday and on which she'd circled their route. 'We head down the main road and veer off down Muong Hoa Street and that's where we'll come to the ticket booth to pay our entry fee into the rice fields. Easy-peasy.'

'A RAMBLING WE WILL go, a rambling we will go, hey ho a derry-o, a rambling we will go.' Moira had found herself singing this silently as she put one boot in front of the other. Mammy was a few steps ahead of her, whistling as she traversed the terraced paths on their itinerary. She reminded Moira of one of Snow White's little helpers and she half expected her to have grown a white beard by the time she turned around next. She was in her element, map in hand, a natural leader and it would have been really annoying if she hadn't shaken off her foul mood just as Mammy had said she would. The clean, sharp air had cleared her head half an hour or so back and their surroundings were far too beautiful for anyone to stay grumpy for long.

They wound their way through the fields, the terraced ridges splaying down the hillside in a mosaic of green and gold. They'd passed by lots of small walking groups all of whom had a guide leading the way. Mammy had whispered to Moira that they obviously weren't ramblers if they needed someone to show them the way. Moira didn't want to burst her bubble by mentioning that her clueless tourists probably kept whole families here fed and clothed with the fee they'd paid their guides. When they came to a fork on the trail the cluster of water-bottle toting people they'd been shadowing turned left.

'We'll head off to the right, Moira, get away from the crowds and according to the map there should be a village we can visit an hour or so from here.' She took her reading glasses off and popped them back in her jacket pocket before folding the map up and putting it away too.

Moira felt the left heel of her boot beginning to rub. She thought this walk was going to be a picnic, that's what Mammy had said. An hour or so away did not make for a picnic in her book but first things first. 'Mammy, have you got plasters because I'm after starting with a blister?'

'Sure, you'll be grand, Moira.'

If she heard that one more time...

'We'll crack on a little ways further and then have a rest; I'll sort you out with one then.'

There was no point arguing so Moira took a moment to click away with her camera at the vista of picturesque wooden houses dotted in the distance before, trying not to think about her sore heel, she hurried after her mammy.

It was beginning to get quite warm she thought as they wound their way up higher and higher into mountainous countryside. Mind that could be down to the exercise as much as any change in the actual temperature. She gave a grateful sigh when Mammy at last held her hand up and announced they would have a scroggin break. A few ticks later Moira snatched the plaster from her and tended to her reddening heel. She followed it by drinking deeply from her water bottle and helping herself to a handful of the scroggin. The way Mammy was talking it up she was expecting a surge of renewed energy as she munched on the superfoods but five minutes after swallowing, she felt exactly the same. She hoped she didn't wind up constipated from the peanuts, they were good for that.

'How much further to the village, Mammy?'

'Ah sure, it's not far away now.'

'Will it be uphill all the way?'

'It's only a little slope, Moira, you'll be grand.'

Famous fecking last words, Moira thought, eyeing the black clouds that were banding together overhead. The sun had disappeared and in the few minutes they'd been resting the temperature had dropped too. 'Look up there.' She pointed to the ominous sky. 'It looks like it's going to pour. Maybe we should turn back?'

'What's that thing you're wearing?'

'A jacket.'

'What sorta jacket, Moira?'

'A rain jacket.'

'I rest my case. Now c'mon the sooner we get moving the sooner we'll get to the village. We can shelter there for a while if it gets heavy but I don't think it will come to much and anyway you won't melt. A bit of rain never hurt anyone. Anyone would think I was in my twenties and you had sixty-year-old bones the way you're carrying on.'

Moira did a rude finger sign behind her mammy's back.

BY MOIRA'S RECKONING they'd been walking for at least an hour and the air had been growing steadily heavier and cooler. Her blister had erupted too despite the plaster. She was convinced they'd taken a wrong turning somewhere along the way because surely, they should have been at the village now. There were no signs of life around them and the terrain had changed. They'd long since moved away from the rice terraces and onto a track fit for a mountain goat. The foliage had thickened on either side of them too. It was madness to keep going she thought as a fat drop of rain splatted on her head.

It was swiftly followed by three more. 'Right, that's it, Mammy I'm making an executive decision. The heavens are about to open and this track will turn to mud when they do. It's been a glorious walk.' That was overdoing it, she'd had enough an hour and a half ago. 'But it's time to turn back.'

Maureen frowned. She was a determined woman and as a proud rambler she was struggling to admit to herself that there was a strong possibility she had indeed misread the map. The rambler motto was 'Not all who wanders is lost,' but in this case she thought they might well be.

There was a hissing as the rain began to sheet in earnest. It dripped off Maureen's nose as she conceded that yes, this was ridiculous. It was time to go back to town. It was hard to believe now that they'd begun the day with glorious sunshine, she thought, silently setting off back the way they'd come. Her shoulders slumped with defeat. It was going to be a long and sodden walk back to town.

Moira felt the track liquefying beneath her feet and as her boots squelched deeper with each step, she poked her tongue out at Mammy. She'd only worn these boots once and they'd be destroyed by the time she got back to the hotel. Not that she had any intention of doing anything that might require hiking boots ever again. She'd toss the fecking things out when they got back to the hotel. And, she was definitely getting first shower. Trust Mammy to have to go against the grain and turn the opposite way to every other tourist on the mountainside.

Maureen was not happy either. This was not what she'd had in mind. Nor was it anything remotely like she'd envisaged all those times as she'd tramped around the Howth hills. By now she and Moira should have been sipping tea in the village and munching on something hot and tasty. She'd hoped to buy a bit more of the brocade too. She'd planned on timing their return to town through the rice paddies so that they'd be bathed in a photographer's dreamy, late afternoon glow. Instead here they were bumbling about in the pouring rain, getting soaked to the bone, miles from any signs of life. She was so busy huffing with the injustice of it all that she didn't see the rut in the track. Over she went, landing with a sickening crunch.

'Jaysus, Mammy! What did you do?' Moira's voice was shrill as she skidded toward her. She knelt down beside her. Mammy was sitting at an awkward angle, her face white and her eyes huge in her face with shock.

'Oh Sweet Mother of Divine, Moira, I think I'm after breaking something.'

Chapter 34

'Do you think you can walk if I help you?' Moira didn't like the way the beads of sweat had broken out on her mammy's face or how she was shivering, her teeth chattering. The rain kept pouring and opening her pack she retrieved the T-shirt she'd brought in case she got too hot. Fat chance of that she thought wiping the rain from her mammy's face. 'Put your arm around my shoulder and I'll see if we can get you up on your feet.'

Maureen did as she was told and Moira tried to ease her upright but she fell back against the sodden earth with a howl of pain. 'I can't do it, Moira!'

Moira's breath was coming in short steamy puffs as panic began to set in. *This was bad, this was very bad. If Mammy couldn't walk how were they going to get back to town?*

'You're going to have to go and get some help,' Maureen rasped, the pain leaching into her voice.

'I'm not leaving you here alone in this.'

'Moira, you have to. I can't walk and we can't just sit here. We could be here all night if we don't do something.'

Moira knew she was right. Nobody would be out looking for them because nobody knew they were here. She didn't know much about surviving in the great outdoors but she did know hypothermia was a very real risk if they didn't get off this mountainside before the temperatures plummeted, as they would do once it grew dark. She shivered and it wasn't from the

cold it was from fear. They were in a right mess and it was up to
her to get them out of it.

'Go, Moira. Fast as you can.'

Moira kissed her mammy on the forehead and said
somewhat inanely, 'Don't move. I'll be as fast as I can. I love
you, Mammy.' She felt her throat closing over and she
swallowed hard. This wasn't the time for dramatics, she had to
stay focussed and get moving. She didn't look back not wanting
to see Mammy so small and vulnerable as she raced off down
the path. She could do this. Just follow the path all the way
back to the fork where they'd made the mistake of turning
right, and then the path through the terraces back to town. *Be
brave, Moira, be fearless for Mammy's sake. C'mon, girl, you can
do it!*

She jogged along thinking about the story Sally-Ann had
told them and how brave she must have been. Mammy too had
been brave leaving the family fold and going far afield. Brave
women. She was brave too, she told herself just before she
slipped over, feeling her shoulder burn as she hit the ground.

She sat up and took a second to catch her breath. Whatever
she'd just done it was only on the surface. Nothing was broken
and giving her shoulder a quick rub she got up. As she carried
on, she made a promise to HIM upstairs that if she got her
mammy out of this okay then she would do better. She'd be a
better person. A kinder person. She'd help others. Something
else too, she decided as she ploughed on through the mud and
the rain, she'd go to college and do the Fine Arts degree she
should have done all along.

MOIRA HEARD THE VOICES before she saw who they belonged to and finding her voice she bellowed, 'Help!' before picking up her pace and racing toward where they'd come from. The rain had eased and through the mist she saw a small group of trekkers. She'd never been so grateful to see anyone in her life and that's when she began to cry.

Chapter 35

Mammy's Travel Journal

Hello from Noi Bai International Airport, Hanoi. We're on our way home and me with my foot in plaster because, let me tell you, what a dramatic end to the trip we've had. I'll spare you some of the detail but Moira and I set off on our trek through the Sa Pa rice terraces three days ago and somehow found ourselves halfway up Mount Fan Si Pan—only the highest mountain in the country! The weather changed all of a sudden and one minute we'd been happily moseying along in the sunshine, the next it began to pour down. It got very dark too. We'd decided we'd better head back and it was only a few minutes later that I was after taking a tumble. So there we were in the torrential rain up the side of a mountain and me unable to move up or down the track because I'd managed to break my ankle.

It was all a bit of a worry and the only thing for it was for Moira to run off to find help. I didn't want her to leave me on my own but we didn't have a choice and when she'd gone it crossed my mind that I could die there all alone, and that's not one word of a lie. The pain was horrendous, even worse than the childbirth just in a different location obviously. But you know a funny thing happened, I was frozen to the bone so I was and very afraid when all of a sudden, I felt as if someone had tossed a thick blanket around me and that I was wrapped in a warm embrace. I knew *it was Brian he'd come to keep an eye on things until Moira could find help. Everything would be alright, and it was.*

I have to say I was very proud of Moira. I know she was frightened to leave me but she did what she had to do. She proved herself a brave and able girl when it mattered. The thing with Moira is she underestimates herself and her abilities she always has. It's a frustrating thing to watch your child who has so much potential shy away from it instead of striding toward it with both arms wide open. I think knowing she saved the day has given her more confidence. The silver lining in a cloud and something else very good came out of it all. She's decided to go to the college and do her Fine Arts degree. She made me a very happy Mammy when she told me that and it took my mind off the nurse at the hospital taking to my travel pants with a pair of scissors. I'm getting ahead of myself though.

Moira happened upon a group of strapping Danes who came to our rescue. Two of the men made a queen's chair with their hands and carried me back to the town. It's all a bit of a blur but Moira tells me I kept telling them they were fine young fellows. She thinks I must have been delirious. We went to the local hospital but they couldn't set the cast there so we were driven to a hospital some 38km away in Lao Kai. I'd been given pain relief by then so everything was rosy until we got there and the nurse snipped away at my pants. I was disappointed about that but it was the only way they could get the cast on. Moira was marvellous sorting out all the travel insurance. She says we'll claim for the pants.

I spent the night in the hospital and we went back to Sa Pa the next day and spent one more night there before getting the bus back to Hanoi. I've been told we're going to take up a whole row down the back of our plane as I have to keep my ankle elevated. It doesn't hurt so much now more of an ache but I've been keeping up with the pain medication just in case. I can't wait to see Rosemary's face when I tell my story at rambling group, she'll be agape so she will. At least too if it had to happen then at least it happened at the end of our tour.

I don't mind telling you it's been a marvellous trip, broken ankle and all. I am a lucky woman so I am.

MOIRA LOOKED ACROSS at where Mammy was sprawled across the four seats, plaster cast resting on a pillow. She'd already written 'you're a Ten in my book Mammy' on it. The braids were fanned out on the pillow on which her head was resting at the other end of the row. For someone who said she never slept on planes, she was doing a grand impersonation of being out for the count, right down to the soft, contented snores. It was probably the pain medication she was on, Moira mused. She too had the three seats over from Mammy to herself and was enjoying the luxury of stretching out. She couldn't complain with how they'd been treated since Mammy's accident. Everybody had been wonderful right from the moment she'd stumbled across the Danes. She couldn't fault anyone, not even the nurse who'd snipped mammy's pants, and now the cabin staff were giving them the royal treatment too.

What a trip it had been Moira thought glancing down at the elephant pants. She felt different to the girl who'd left Ireland. She was making plans for herself and settling back into her seat she thought about what it would be like going back to college as an adult student. How would she manage? She didn't know for sure but she wasn't frightened. One thing she did know was she'd pay far more attention to the course work than she would have done when she was fresh out of school. Art was her passion, she'd just lost sight of that for a few years. Life, she'd learned on this tour was too short not to follow her dreams. It was a lesson her mammy had taught her because if she hadn't of followed her dream, she could very well be married to yer buck toothed man in Ballyclegg.

THE RED-CARPET TREATMENT continued through duty free where Maureen splashed out on her Arpège and Moira threw caution to the wind and what was left on her credit card by splurging on a bottle of Chanel's Allure. There'd be no treats when she became a poor student. Maureen made noises about how it would have been nice to receive a little extra discount on account of her injury, all the way to Irish customs. It was as Moira handed over their declaration cards that the proverbial carpet was pulled out from under them.

'You've ticked this.' An officious, ruddy-cheeked man stabbed at a box on one of the cards. Moira peered closer; it was to do with wooden products.

'My wood carving, Moira.' Maureen piped up from her wheelchair. Her crutches were resting across her lap and the patient assistant who'd been there to greet them with the chair when they'd disembarked was standing with his hands resting on the handles waiting for them to clear customs. Moira was standing behind the trolley on which their packs were stacked.

'It's in the top of my pack. Moira, don't just stand there. Yer man, here wants to see it.'

Which would be on the bottom of the trolley, Moira thought, her patience wearing thin. Mammy had no right to go on at her for not waking her when the dinner trolley came around; she'd not stopped going on about missing out on her chicken curry with rice for the last hour. The lack of discount from the duty free had been a welcome break from the topic. She heaved her pack onto the ground before crouching down to unlock and unzip Mammy's.

'Moira.' Maureen hissed. 'These two gentlemen do not want to see my smalls.'

'Well you shouldn't have put your canoe inside a pair of them then should you?' Moira unwrapped the offending piece of wood and handed it over. 'It's nothing to do with me,' she said as he took it in his gloved hand and began to inspect it. She hastily did the bag back up and lifted hers back onto the trolley. She was keen to get this last bit over and done with so they could get home now that it was within sniffing distance. Mammy was going to stay with her and Aisling, who was in the dark as to the accident. They'd figure out a way to get her up the stairs, maybe Tom and Quinn could do the Queen's chair lift thing.

The officer held the carving out in front of him, turning it this way and that, a frown forming between his bushy black eyebrows. 'What's this when it's at home then?'

'It's a canoe of course.' Maureen pulled a face at Moira who was biting her lip in an effort not to giggle at the officer's bewildered expression. 'I made it myself.'

'At least you didn't pay for it.' He handed it to Maureen before waving them on their way.

So it was, a strange man wheeled Mammy through to the arrivals area where Aisling who'd been waiting impatiently for them was beginning to wonder if they'd missed their flight. She stopped her anxious fidgeting as she saw a woman in a wheelchair with braided hair like a member of Boney M being pushed through the doors. On her lap she was holding something proudly erect and dear God, thought Aisling surely it wasn't a—

'Aisling.' The woman waved the offending wooden item and the penny dropped as Moira appeared behind her in the elephant pants. She rushed forward to greet them both. 'What's happened, Mammy? Are you alright? And what is that on your lap?'

'It's her wooden p—'

'Moira! That's enough of that. It's a canoe, Aisling, sure, what do you think it is?'

Aisling and Moira's eyes met and they exchanged a look that said they were in mutual agreement as to exactly what it looked like!

'Now then, we'd better let this young man have his chair back, Moira.' She shot her a look which Moira correctly interpreted as give him a little bit of cash which she did, while Mammy ordered Aisling to help her out of the chair. 'I'll tell you all about what we've been up to on the way home. Ooh I'm gasping for a cup of good ole Irish tea and one of Bronagh's custard creams if she'll let us have one.'

Read on for an excerpt from Book 4, Rosi's Regrets
http://mybook.to/TGseriespage

THE BLACK NOSE POKED through the gap under the bricks, twitching as it sniffed the frosty night air. A bristly red head popped through the hole, eyes sweeping the courtyard to check the coast was clear. A strip of light illuminated the familiar path to the rubbish bin; his bin. The beam was shining through the gap, where the curtains hadn't quite been closed in the room directly over this outdoor area. It might only be a short distance across the concreted ground to his destination but it was one fraught with potential landmines. One big one in particular who waved a rolling pin and screamed louder than he could! Satisfied the cook who had it in for him was long gone for the day, the little red fox squeezed his body through the hole. It was harder work than usual, he'd been eating well of late. But he was nothing if not determined and after one good push, out he popped.

He padded across to the bin, a sniper with his target in sight, a bin where a myriad of treats added a splash of variety to a fox's diet and a layer of padding around his middle. A noise broke the silence and he froze, statue-like, ears pricked on high alert. He didn't move, prepared to wait it out until he knew what had made the sound. An acrid smoky smell danced over the high walls surrounding the courtyard. It would be the man next door; he would be puffing on that smelly stick he so loved while the woman in the house shrieked it was high time he gave the things away. She would tell the man he'd catch his death standing around in the cold and the man would reply, 'If a man who'd worked hard all his life could partake of the one pleasure he had left inside, then he wouldn't catch his death.' She'd shout back that he could 'Fecking well freeze.'

The little red fox didn't like their backyard, it wasn't worth visiting. There was never anything worthwhile in their bin. Not like here; this was the piece de resistance of rubbish bins. His tongue poked out as he carried on his stealthy path to where, if he was lucky, he might find a sliver of black pudding, or even better white pudding, bacon rind, and soda bread. If there was an award for rubbish bins this one would get the Oscar. He reached it and began to salivate as he stretched up to nose the lid off with well-practised ease, and as it clattered to the ground he worked fast. His luck was in, white pudding! It was a night to celebrate, indeed! He nose-dived gleefully into the bin and retrieved it, snaffling it down. There was bacon rind too, oh yes he was fine dining tonight. He was about to go in for seconds when the window above the courtyard squeaked open. A man, with a mean thin face which looked angrier than the rolling pin woman's, peered out.

The fox didn't like the look of him. He meant business and although it broke his heart to leave, he scarpered across that courtyard to the safety of the gap under the wall. A splash of icy water hit his tail as he pushed his way back through from where he'd come, the midnight garden beyond the wall.

The man with the thin, pinched face shook his head and wrenched the window back down. Vermin, no better than rats those things. He put the empty glass down on the bedside table and got back into bed. He'd have words with the manager in the morning. The girl with the mane of red-gold hair and silly shoes. Oh yes, he'd be telling her: for the ridiculous sums of money he was being charged for the dubious privilege of staying in this establishment, O'Mara's needed to up its standards.

Chapter 1

London 1999

Roisin twisted the plain gold band on her finger and stared at the statement lying open in front of her. There were two sharp creases across the piece of paper where it had been folded inside the envelope and she smoothed them hoping that the action might magically erase the information neatly set out before her. It didn't of course and she blinked trying to convince herself she hadn't read what was laid out in neat, black font but when she re-focused the words were the same as they'd been a split-second ago.

The table at which she was sitting still wore the debris from breakfast—from normal day to day life. A puddle of milk left behind by Noah who'd been craning his neck trying to catch sight of the cartoon he'd left blaring in the living room as he shovelled in cornflakes. Dirty dishes waited to be cleared and toast crumbs kept the puddle company as they waited to be wiped up. The postcards Noah had received from Mammy and Moira sent from their Vietnam holiday were resting against the salt and pepper shakers.

Speaking of Noah, he'd left the television on and it was almost but not quite drowned out by the kitchen radio which Roisin had tuned to BBC 1. It was her routine to change the station over from the newsy BBC World Colin preferred of a morning the moment he shut the front door behind him.

She was dimly aware of an annoyingly preppy pop hit, currently storming the charts, playing. It seemed at odds with what she'd just discovered. Beethoven's classic da-da-da-duuum from *Symphony No. 5* would have been more appropriate.

She stopped twisting her ring, only to find it felt like the precious metal was branding her. The sensation, she knew was in her head but it felt real and unable to stand it she wrested the band from her finger before dropping it on the table. She watched as it rocked and rolled like a penny piece before finally giving up its dance. Her finger looked naked without its gold adornment. She'd stopped wearing her engagement ring eons ago. The marquise cut diamond had been a stunning choice but it had proven to be an impractical one. She'd constantly snagged her tights, pulled sweaters, and in the end, when Noah had been born, terrified she'd scratch him with it she'd put it back in its box and tucked it away down the back of her knicker drawer. If Colin had noticed she'd stopped wearing it he'd never commented.

Roisin didn't know where the impractical gene she'd been bestowed with had come from but making fanciful decisions was the story of her life. Not once in her thirty-six years had anyone said, 'Gosh that Roisin O'Mara is a practical girl,' or 'Sure, Rosi O'Mara's full of sensible ideas, so she is.' She'd never been the girl people turned to for sage advice or the person you'd rely on to hold you steady through one of life's storms. It wasn't that she was unreliable as such, and she was fiercely loyal when it came to family and friends, it was just she was what Mammy liked to call a little bit airy-fairy.

If you were to ask Maureen O'Mara to sum up her three daughters, Rosi knew exactly what she'd say. Moira, her baby, was a prima donna who thought she'd been born with a silver spoon in her mouth. She hadn't, although in Roisin's opinion she was spoilt and got away with a lot more than her three siblings ever had. Aisling, the changeling with her red-gold hair was one of life's peacemakers and she spent far too much time sorting out other people's problems while ignoring her own. A bit of an ostrich was Aisling. As for Rosi, her eldest daughter, well, Mammy would say, she'd been a pain in the arse teenager—all attitude and such but, one thing was for sure, she'd been born with her head in the clouds. Anyone would think the milkman had had a hand in things when it came to her girls, she'd lament laughingly to anyone listening, if it weren't for the fact Aisling took after her father's side of the family, God rest his soul. Rosi and Moira were the dark haired, olive skinned spits of their dear mammy.

Annoyingly, and a little unfairly in Roisin's opinion, Mammy never included her only son and eldest child, Patrick in this equation because to her mind, she could sum him up on one word, 'perfect'. It irked all three of the sisters because he was far from it but she of all people knew love was blind. She also knew, since becoming a mammy herself, that you'd forgive your children anything, even for being an arsey, vain, eejit like her brother was.

Roisin thought she'd made a proper, practical, grown-up choice when she'd said yes to Colin's proposal. It had come about after a very impractical decision—forgetting to use a condom. He'd been very old-fashioned about the whole business, quietly ringing her dad to ask if he'd give his daughter's hand in marriage before popping the question. Seeing as Roisin was over thirty and pregnant, Brian would have bitten his hand off had he done this in person, or at the very least thrown a dowry at him, but it had been done over the telephone and so far as she knew no money had exchanged hands. So, with her father's permission and unbeknown to her, the rest of the O'Mara clan were eagerly awaiting a further telephone call to confirm her engagement; Colin had taken her out for a meal in a posh London eatery.

It was somewhere in between the main and dessert he'd gotten down on bended knee. At first she'd been unsure what he was up to. He'd leaped out of his seat, crouched down and looked very red in the face. She'd wondered if he'd been seized by cramp and contemplated getting down beside him and rubbing his leg to try and ease it but then dessert had arrived as he simultaneously asked if she'd like to marry him.

In hindsight Roisin didn't know if she'd been so quick to say yes because she wanted to get stuck into her crème brûlée. She was four months pregnant and dessert really, really mattered to her. She'd managed to hold back long enough for Colin to open a red velvet box and found herself blinking at the sparkle. Inside the box nestled a diamond ring. It was exactly like the one she'd pointed out in the window of the jewellers as being the sort of thing she'd like *were* they ever to get engaged. She didn't trust Colin's taste and had a feeling if she wasn't clear about what she wanted she could very well wind up being offered his great granny's hideous heirloom opal if he decided to make an honest woman of her.

The thing was though, she'd thought, torn between the glittering stone and the golden sugary crust of her brûlée, saying yes wasn't just about her. There was little bean too. This was not the time to be flighty and act on the spur of the moment, nor, she told herself sternly was it the moment to crack that gorgeous crust so she could tuck in. Oh no, this was the time to behave like a sensible, pregnant women. Accordingly she'd paused and taken a moment to run through a mental marriage checklist.

Would Colin be a good husband and father? *Yes, she thought he probably would.*

Would he make a good provider? (Yes, okay it was old-fashioned, but Rosi fully intended to stay at home throughout little bean's formative years and make lots of wholesome, whole foods) *Yes, he was a hard worker and liked to think of himself as one of life's movers and shakers.*

Was he trustworthy? *Well, if he'd lied to her, she didn't know about it.*

Did he love her? *He must do, mustn't he? Just look at the enormous blingy ring he was offering her.*

Did she love him? *Yes, she thought she did, not that she had much experience of being in love but he made her feel safe and while it wasn't the grand passion she'd seen in films, he was steady and reliable and there was a lot to be said for that when you had a little bean on the way.*

Accordingly as Colin began to grimace from spending so long balancing on one knee, Roisin had accepted the ring and beamed that yes she'd love to marry him. All the while she'd been eyeing the crème brûlée and thinking to herself *righty-ho, let's get this show on the road.* The custard dessert had been delicious too, when much to her relief he'd finally slid the ring on her finger and she'd been able to thwack that toasted sugar with the back of her spoon.

That had been nearly six years ago. She hadn't eaten crème brûlée since, she realised wondering how she'd gotten it so wrong? She picked up the bank statement that had thrown her morning into a complete tizz. Without thinking she screwed it up into a ball and threw it at the wall.

Chapter 2

'Mummy.' There was the sound of little feet pattering down the stairs. 'I've brushed my teeth and been to the toilet. I'm ready.'

Roisin pushed her chair back and got up from her seat. 'And washed your hands?' The question burst forth automatically. Her world might have just crashed down around her but she would have to pick her way through the rubble and take Noah to school. Life had to go on. There would be time to think about what she was going to do when she got home. She looked at his face and reading his expression sighed. 'Noah, how many times do I have to tell you? We go through this same routine every morning.'

His little face looked petulant and she could see him weighing up the odds as to whether he should make a fuss for fuss's sake or whether he should do as he was told. He'd been making a fuss lots lately. For his sake, she was hoping he would choose the latter, she didn't trust herself not to lose patience with him this morning. She never thought she had it in her to be a fisherwoman until she'd had a small child whom she loved more than life itself but who also had an amazing ability to bring out her inner fishwife. Mind you she'd thought she'd put homemade vegetable purees in his baby bird mouth when he went on solids and handwash all his nappies too. Look how that had gone!

There must have been something about her expression because Noah turned and ran back up the stairs. Roisin stood rooted to the spot and without thinking embarked on a round of the breathing exercises she'd been shown. She took a long slow breath in through her nose feeling the air fill her lower lungs and then her upper lungs. She held it there for a count of three before exhaling through pursed lips, trying to relax her facial muscles, jaw, shoulders and stomach, as her yoga teacher Harriet had demonstrated. She'd have liked to have practiced her forward bend because sitting on the floor with head resting on her knees while she held onto her toes had a surprisingly calming effect on her but there was no time for that. Nor could she meditate herself off into another zone. Instead she picked up her house keys, shrugged into her coat and, as Noah raced backed down the stairs, she wrapped a scarf around her neck.

She grabbed hold of her son. 'Coat!' She picked it up off the back of the chair where it had been slung yesterday afternoon and held it open for him. He shoved his arms inside it before picking up his school bag and heading for the front door, urging his mummy on, 'I can't be late. I don't want to miss show and tell. Charlie Wentworth-Islington-Greene is bringing her pet gerbil, Beyoncé in today.'

Chapter 3

Roisin was only half listening to Noah's steady stream of chatter as they crunched through the last of the leaves under an arbour of stripped trees toward Clover Hill Primary. Her heart had returned to its normal rate of beats per minute after the awful barky Alsatian had reared up at them. It did the same thing every morning and it never ceased to startle her when it appeared, paws resting on the top of the front gate, saliva dripping from its mouth, ruffing furiously at them. The dog always managed to startle her but this morning she'd had enough. She would not allow herself to be intimidated anymore. So, instead of hurrying past, she stood her ground glaring back at the dog, daring him to do his worst. He'd carried on for a second or two longer and then jumped back down, tail wagging as he wandered off around the garden to his cock his leg or whatever party trick he had planned next.

Noah high-fived her, and she felt proud like she'd just given him one of those really important life lessons. Her son had really blossomed in confidence these last months, ever since he'd started attending the exclusive primary, or so his teacher had told her at the Meet the Teacher evening. It seemed to her he was a different boy when he was at school.

Children did not come with an instruction manual, that was for sure, and Mammy had said to her not long after Noah was born that raising a child was one big phase after another and that probably the best bit came around the middle years, eleven and twelve. It was a reprieve before the horrible teenage bit. She'd given Roisin the hairy eyeball as she said that, before adding, 'and then when they grow out of that all you can hope for is that somehow you've managed to raise a good person who can stand on their own two feet.' Her mammy's words echoed in her head because that was what frightened Roisin now—could she stand on her own two feet? It felt like ever such a long time since she'd had to and frankly she hadn't been all that good at it when she had.

Noah's behaviour had deteriorated at home lately and she suspected the atmosphere between her and Colin was the catalyst. There were lots of barbed comments in lowered voices and if she were being honest she would say it was because they just didn't like each other very much these days. Things couldn't go on the way they had been. It wasn't fair on Noah. *Oh what a great big, fecking mess.* If it were just her she'd have packed her bags a long time ago but it wasn't just her and Noah was Colin's son too.

If anyone were to ask, Roisin would say he loved his son but he expected a lot of his little boy, too much in her opinion. She flashed back to the toddler football matches where her husband would stand on the side lines shouting—he was a man who liked to win. The tips and tricks he'd bombard his son with at half time had seen him start refusing to go of a Saturday morning. She'd tried to talk to Colin about it but he'd said it was down to Noah, and that he needed to toughen up.

A car raced past them farting out exhaust fumes and Roisin scowled and muttered, 'Slow down you eejit.' She wished Noah would let her hold his hand but he insisted he was too big for that now he was at school. She still wasn't used to the hole his not being home between nine and three had left in her days. The idea of having all that glorious time to herself used to seem so tantalising on those days when she was up to her ears in Lego and Play-Doh, the reality however was quite different. Their Victorian semi seemed overly large and full of echoes when it was just her rattling around in it. She hadn't realised until he'd started school how reliant she'd become on her son for company. Colin was rarely home before eight these days and when he was home they weren't very nice to each other. She missed her sisters and her mammy and the noisy, coming and goings of the O'Mara's household growing up.

She, Colin and Noah lived in a house chosen for its smart postcode, something that had been very important to her husband even if it had stretched them financially, just as Noah's school fees were doing. Appearances mattered to her husband. It was the world in which he moved. Sometimes she wondered what it was he'd seen in her apart from that initial physical attraction because they were opposites in so many aspects of their personalities. 'Things' had never really mattered to Roisin or at least they hadn't. Now, the thought of having nothing terrified her. She knew it was becoming a mum that had wrought that change in her, that and the years spent with Colin listening to his big talk.

Roisin caught the word, 'gerbil' as Noah tugged at her coat sleeve. 'Mum, you're not listening to me.' His little face looked hurt and she felt a pang of guilt.

'Sorry, sweetheart. Tell me again.'

He did that thing with his mouth that Colin did when he was annoyed before replying. 'I *said*, do you think gerbils eat toast?'

Roisin was almost afraid to ask. 'Why, darling?'

'Because I've got a piece in my pocket I saved from breakfast.' Noah said this as though it should be obvious and make perfect sense for him to have stashed a piece of toast in his pocket.

Roisin chewed her lip, biting back a sigh because, knowing her luck, it would be a piece slathered in sticky marmalade. Mrs Flaherty, the O'Mara's guesthouse cook always weighed his mammy down with jars of her homemade jam when she came to visit. She knew how partial Roisin was to her jam having caught her more than once as a child with her finger in the pot. Indeed, Roisin had been like Pooh Bear was to honey with Mrs Flaherty's sweet marmalade. Now, she tried not to envisage her son's gooey shorts pocket as she replied, 'Hmm, well I'm no expert when it comes to gerbils, Noah, but I think they eat leafy lettuce sort-a things. It might pay to check with Charlie before you feed, er Beyoncé.' An image of a gerbil lying flat on its back with its little legs stiff in the air sprang to mind and she shook it away. Her son being responsible for the offing of Charlie Wentworth-Islington-Greene's gerbil she did not need, not on top of what she'd discovered this morning.

They rounded the corner and spied the usual swarm of parents ahead, along with the shiny cars that were far too big for the narrow road they were vying for space on. Noah picked up his pace and despite everything, the sight of his little legs pumping along made her smile; she was lucky he loved going to school. There were some children who clung sobbing to their mummies of a morning and Roisin always felt so sad for them both, knowing how hard she'd find it if Noah were to do the same.

'Morning, Roisin,' an attractive woman clad in exercise gear with her hair pulled back in a ponytail called out. 'Are you going to Harriet's this morning?'

'Hi, Nessa.' She managed a wan smile in her direction. "No, not this morning. I'm feeling a bit under the weather will you pass on my apologies to her.'

'Oh dear. Well I hope you feel better soon.' She took a step back as though frightened she might catch whatever lurgy Roisin was incubating.

Yoga with Harriet would have done her good this morning, Roisin mused, following Noah's lead to the gates. It would have calmed her down and helped her think about what she was going to do in a rational manner. She couldn't go though, she needed to head home and face up to what Colin had done and, if she were honest, it was easier to stay angry than to try and make sense of it all. 'Bye, bye, love.' She kissed the top of Noah's head. 'Have a good day, I'll see you at home time.' He had no idea how much his little world was about to change and the thought made her feel physically sick.

It was a relief to be distracted by his excited squeal as he caught sight of Charlotte standing lopsided with her pet cage in hand. She was looking impatient as her mother, Stephanie, tightened the band on one of her pigtails before giving her a kiss goodbye. 'Noah, remember to ask Charlie before you try and feed Beyoncé.' Her words fell on deaf ears as he propelled himself through the huddle of mums toward the little girl.

Roisin's gaze settled on the group of women she called the SLOB gang clustered outside the entrance as though guarding it. They were smiling and chatting in voices designed to carry. Tiff Cooper-Jones caught her eye and mouthed. 'Coffee?'

Roisin shook her head and shouted over, 'No, not today, Tiff, I'm feeling a bit sick.'

The other woman's pert nose curled. 'Oh, well best keep your distance, you don't want to spread it whatever it is.' She turned back to her cronies.

Roisin mentally poked her tongue out at her. She'd rather be afflicted with multiple cold sores than join her and her pals for coffee. SLOB stood for Soy Latte, Obnoxious Bitches. To her shame it was a group that she hovered on the periphery of, occasionally joining them for a cup after they'd waved their offspring goodbye instead of heading for her usual destination, Harriet's yoga studio. She was only invited on the basis of Colin having a working connection with Tiff's husband and didn't know why she bothered going because she always came away from their gatherings feeling annoyed and out of sorts. The only thing she could put her inability to ignore them completely down to was her mammy having told her years ago that it was better to keep your enemies close.

Over to one side and definitely on the outer fringe was Lily—she was not the norm here at Clover Hill. A top fashion model, she was very beautiful but a little rough around the edges having grown up on a council estate. Lily had a smouldering cigarette permanently attached to her hand as part of her Weight Watchers plan. Roisin didn't exactly approve of her smoking at the school gates, it wasn't a good look but so long as she didn't blow the smoke in her and Noah's direction she couldn't see how it affected her. She wasn't the judgmental sort, live and let live had always been her motto. There was a part of her that secretly admired Lily for not caring what the other mothers thought of her. She knew the SLOB gang called her Fag Ash Lil behind her back and were all in silent awe of her jutting hipbones.

Roisin wished she could adopt the same kind of aloofness but she was too sensitive for that. She'd even found herself espousing on Noah's burgeoning musical gift—he'd recently undertaken recorder lessons—in direct competition with Tiff who was convinced her daughter was the next Charlotte Church. She hadn't liked herself for it much and had wondered why she'd felt the need to enter the arena with Tiff. The odds were never going to be in her favour. Besides, she was proud of Noah for just being Noah and truth be told every time he announced he was going to practice that fecking instrument, Roisin flinched. She never used to be like that. Easy-osi Rosi, her sisters used to call her.

Her gaze flicked from one SLOB member to another. Their husbands wouldn't have kissed them goodbye that morning with guilty consciences. Well that wasn't strictly true, Claire Stanford's husband might have been feeling guilty. The word had gone round the last time she'd sat sipping her frothy brew, that the reason Claire hadn't shown her face at school all week was because she'd found out he was having it off with his secretary. There'd been lots of tutting about what a cliché he was in between mouthfuls of scones or muffins.

Oh Jaysus! Roisin shuddered despite the warmth of her coat. Would she be the subject of their tittle-tattle when it got out what Colin had done? And it would get out, it was inevitable. Gossip was like water. It found its way through everything eventually. She could imagine the juicy story would have them salivating for days. 'And Roisin had no idea, imagine that?' It wasn't fecking well fair! Their days were panning out so normally whereas hers, since she'd found the bundle of letters shoved in the glove box of their Merc, the Merc she hardly ever drove, had imploded.

Book 4, The Guesthouse on the Green Series

Rosi's Regrets

'BEST BOOKS I'VE READ for years. Reminds me of Maeve Binchy!' *Reader Review*

'I'm loving the O'Mara girls and of course their hysterical Mammy!' *Reader Review*

Every guest who comes to stay at O'Mara's Guesthouse in Dublin has a story to tell. The little red fox who visits the bins in the courtyard has a tale of his own as do the long serving staff, and the O'Mara family themselves have had their fair share of ups and downs too...

Roisin O'Mara. Rosi regrets a lot of things. She regrets having just scoffed the out-of-date chocolate bar she found down the bottom of her bag, and the cheese she ate before bed the night before—it gave her the strangest dreams. Her mammy always told her not to eat cheese before bed. She should have listened. Just like she should have listened when she asked her if she was sure doing the right thing getting married because that's her biggest regret of all.

When Rosi discovers a secret her husband's been keeping, she hightails it back to the family fold in Dublin. It's not just about her though, there's their son Noah to think about too, and Rosi's not sure she's strong enough to stand on her own two feet.

Reggie Nolan has regrets too. Saying sorry, isn't in his vocabulary but time's running out. He's come to stay at O'Mara's to try and find the strength to put things right with the person he loves most in the world.

With a little sisterly love and some advice from her Mammy will Roisin be able to move forward? And can Reggie make amends for what he did thirty years ago, before it's too late?

Manufactured by Amazon.ca
Bolton, ON

24196682R00146